Praise for Richard T. Ry
Adventure

CW01507371

The Vatican Cameos

Winner of the Underground Book Reviews' "Novel of the Year" Award. Winner Silver Medal in the Readers' Favorite book-award contest.

"[*The Vatican Cameos* is] an extravagantly imagined and beautifully written Holmes story." – Lee Child, NY Times Bestselling author and the creator of Jack Reacher

"Once you've read *The Vatican Cameos*, you'll find yourself eagerly awaiting the next in Ryan's series." – Fran Wood, What Fran's Reading for nj.com

"Richard Ryan channels Dan Brown as well as Conan Doyle in this successful novel." – Tom Turley, Sherlockian author

"If you enjoy deeply researched historical fiction, combined with not one but two mystery/thriller stories, then you will really enjoy this excellent Sherlock Holmes pastiche." – Craig Copland, author of New Sherlock Holmes Mysteries

"A great addition to the Holmes Canon. Definitely worth a read." – Rob Hart, author of *The Warehouse* and the Ash McKenna series

"*The Vatican Cameos* opens with a familiar feel for fans of Arthur Conan Doyle's original Sherlock Holmes stories. The plotting is clever, and the alternating stories well-told." – Crime Thriller Hound

The Stone of Destiny

"Sometimes a book comes along that absolutely restores your faith in reading. Such is the 'found manuscript' of Dr. Watson, *The Stone of Destiny*. Exhilarating, superb narrative and a cast of characters that are as dark as they are vivid. ... A thriller of the very first rank." – Ken Bruen, author of *The Guards*, *The Magdalen Martyrs,* and many other novels, as well as the creator of the Jack Taylor series

"A wonderful read for both the casual Sherlock Holmes fan and the most die-hard devotees of the beloved character." – Terrence McCauley, author of *A Conspiracy of Ravens* and *A Murder of Crows*

"Somewhere Sir Arthur Conan Doyle is smiling. Ryan's *The Stone of Destiny* is a fine addition to the Canon." – Reed Farrel Coleman, NY Times Bestselling author of *What You Break*

"Ryan's Holmes is the real deal in [*The Stone of Destiny*]. One hopes the author is hard at work on the next adventure in this wonderfully imagined and executed series." – Fran Wood, What Fran's Reading for nj.com

"Mystery lovers will enjoy reading *The Stone of Destiny: A Sherlock Holmes Adventure* by Richard T. Ryan." – Michelle Stanley, Readers' Choice Awards

"Richard Ryan's prose flows as easily as a stream in the summer. I thought the way the Stone was stolen, how it was transported out of England under the very noses of the army of police, and its hiding place in Ireland were brilliant!" – Raven Reviews

The Druid of Death

"The clever solution, which echoes one from a golden age classic, is the book's best feature." – Publishers Weekly

"*The Druid of Death* is clever and fun, a winning combination. The setting — Victorian England — and the Druidic lore are absolutely captivating. This is my favorite kind of mystery." – Criminal Element

"… the Druidic detail and the depiction of 19th-century London are fascinating and delightful." – Kirkus Reviews

"Ryan creates a thoroughly enjoyable pastiche, giving readers just what you'd expect from such a mystery. The suspense is tangible, and the detection methodologies quirky. He's right on the money with his characterizations of all the usual players, especially Holmes and Watson." – Barbara Searles @thebibliophage.com

"A stunning achievement!" – Ken Bruen, author of *The Guards* and creator of Jack Taylor

"As one would expect from a Sherlock Holmes story, the Great Detective's intellect, keen eye for observation, and logical deductions all play a factor in the satisfying conclusion of this mystery." – Kristopher Zgorski, founder of BOLO Books

"Sherlockians craving a new challenge for their favorite sleuth need look no further than Richard T. Ryan's *The Druid of Death*, which puts Holmes on the trail of one of his most fiendish adversaries ever." – Steven Hockensmith, author of the Edgar Award finalist *Holmes on the Range*

The Merchant of Menace

Short-listed for the annual Drunken Druid Award.

"Oh, what a joy it is to meet Sherlock Holmes and Dr. Watson again! *The Merchant of Menace* is an exciting adventure of priceless valuables, great detective work and just the kind of devilish adversary we love to read about." – Mattias Boström, author of *From Holmes to Sherlock: The Story of the Men and Women Who Created an Icon*

"This rousing, intriguing, devilishly fun caper, well-executed and well-paced, had me hooked from the first page. The dutiful Watson, Holmes' deductive skills, and a worthy nemesis to rival the evil Moriarty himself, make this cat-and-mouse adventure a page-turning, edge-of-your-seat roller-coaster ride well worth taking." – Tracy Clark, author of *Broken Places* and *Borrowed Time* and the creator of Cass Raines

"[*The Merchant of Menace* is] an absolute humdinger of a novel …It is beautifully written, erudite and hugely entertaining." – Ken Bruen, the author of *The Ghosts of Galway* and the creator of Jack Taylor

"The wonderfully titled *The Merchant of Menace* has all the familiarity of a lost Holmesian tale. An enjoyable adventure from the ever-reliable Richard T. Ryan." – Crime Thriller Hound

"With an intriguing premise and a cunning plot, *The Merchant of Menace* will delight Sherlockians of all stripes. Richard T. Ryan has given us a gripping mystery and a loving tribute to the Great Detective." – Daniel Stashower, author of *Teller of Tales: The Life of Arthur Conan Doyle*

Through a Glass Starkly

"Deftly blending Conan Doyle and Dan Brown, Richard Ryan's *Through a Glass Starkly* offers an intriguing mix of history and mystery. Remaining true to the Canon in his depictions of the iconic Holmes and Watson, Ryan also delivers a mystery that should satisfy even the most demanding Sherlockian." – Robert Dugoni, NY Times Bestselling author of *The Eighth Sister* and the creator of Tracy Crosswhite

"Ryan's Watsonian voice is superb, and as with his earlier novels the author has included several affectionate nods to the characters, stories, and intrigues of the original Canon. These twists and turns make this an engrossing and enjoyable read, as do the variety of colourful locations chosen for the action. From a secret *pied-a-terre* in Paris, to the Whispering Gallery in St. Paul's Cathedral, we are carried along at a frenetic pace. I previously read, and thoroughly enjoyed, *The Druid of Death*. *Through a Glass Starkly* is even better!" – Sherlock Holmes Society of London

"Another brilliant addition to the Sherlock Holmes Canon." – Bruce Robert Coffin, author of the Detective Byron mysteries

"Slap on your deerstalker and grab a pipe, Richard Ryan's Sherlock Holmes strikes again. With head-scratching twists and puzzling turns, even Arthur Conan Doyle would be hard-pressed to solve this mystery. *Through a Glass Starkly* will satisfy even the most ardent Holmes fans." – Jean M. Roberts @thebookdelight,com and author of *The Heron*

"Richard T. Ryan does it again with *Through a Glass Starkly*, his latest pastiche featuring Sir Arthur Conan Doyle's legendary team of Holmes and Watson. It is an engrossing, twisty, delicious adventure involving a missing priceless codex, Europe on the verge of war, a mysterious woman, and shadowy figures roaming the London docks. Great fun! – Tracy Clark, author of the Cass Raines Chicago mystery series

Three May Keep a Secret

"Richard T. Ryan's *Three May Keep a Secret* [is] a pitch-perfect adventure that pits Conan Doyle's great detective against a master criminal...It's a tale of fabulous jewels, brilliant forgeries, cunning disguises and a Watson double-act that will make every writer who's ever penned a Holmes pastiche green with 'Why didn't I think of that?'" – Jeffrey Hatcher, screenwriter for *Mr. Holmes*

"Richard Ryan has yet again given us one of his well-crafted yet exciting and entertaining novels of Sherlock Holmes. Settle in for several hours of fun reading." – Robert Katz, MD, BSI

"… the book's strengths, including the imaginative setup, make Ryan's taking up Conan Doyle's mantle again welcome. Fans of traditional pastiches will enjoy this." – Publishers Weekly

"The tour de force in the book is the presence of a criminal mastermind, a worthy replacement for Professor Moriarty, whose shadows are broodingly present in the adventure." – *Sherlock Holmes Society of India*

"Oh man, this was an intense cat-and-mouse game and I loved it! It was really well-written and well-researched … I loved the banter between Holmes and Watson, and as always I liked how every little thing that Holmes does has a purpose. And of course his exceptional deduction skills are always on point!" – Book blogger thereadingowlvina (Elvina Ulrich)

"*Three May Keep a Secret* is a beautifully written, accurately researched and very intriguing Sherlock Holmes pastiche written in the style of Sir Arthur Conan Doyle. Could not put it down once I had started; Sherlock Holmes fans will love this." – Sandra Fabiani, co-creator of HolmesCon

The Poisoned Pawn

"Richard Ryan has again penned another fast paced and carefully plotted pastiche. The characterizations are both strong and canonical. The story is replete with the requisite twists and turns, intriguing villains, and surprise endings. It moves quickly, establishes the necessary atmosphere, and maintains the quality that he's long developed." – Robert Katz, MD, BSI

"An absorbing narrative with a devilish plot – top marks for Richard T. Ryan's latest novel which captures the true spirit of Conan Doyle." – Mark Mower, author of *Sherlock Holmes: The Baker Street Archive*

"It's indeed a pleasure to read a novel in which Professor Moriarty is pulling the strings of another criminal from behind the scenes. In *The Poisoned Pawn*, Richard T. Ryan has the professor maneuver a villain seeking personal revenge into a deadly game against Sherlock Holmes. A rousing adventure from start to finish!" — Ray Riethmeier, editor of *Sherlock Holmes: Stranger Than Truth* and *Sherlock Holmes: Stranger Than Fiction*

"Checkmate! Rich Ryan's depiction of Holmes and Watson never fails to satisfy those of us eager for a new adventure. It's not surprising that he has another winner on his hands!" – Francine Kitts, BSI, ASH

"Fans of Sherlock Holmes, both young and older, will enjoy Richard T. Ryan's entertaining tale of *The Poisoned Pawn* from chapter to chapter, anxiously awaiting for what comes next! Very well researched and detailed! Sit back and enjoy!" – Greg D. Ruby, BSI, ASH, The SOB in Charge The Sherlockians of Baltimore

The Devil's Disciples:
A Sherlock Holmes Adventure

by Richard T. Ryan

First edition published in 2023
© Copyright 2023 Richard T Ryan

The right of Richard T Ryan to be identified as the author of this
work has been asserted by him in accordance with the Copyright,
Designs and Patents Act 1998.

All rights reserved. No reproduction, copy or transmission of
this publication may be made without express prior written
permission. No paragraph of this publication may be reproduced,
copied or transmitted except with express prior written permission
or in accordance with the provisions of the Copyright Act 1956 (as
amended). Any person who commits any unauthorised act in
relation to this publication may be liable to criminal prosecution
and civil claims for damage.

Although every effort has been made to ensure the accuracy of the
information contained in this book, as of the date of publication,
nothing herein should be construed as giving advice. The opinions
expressed herein are those of the author and not of MX Publishing.

Hardcover ISBN 978-1-80424-263-6
Paperback ISBN 978-1-80424-264-3
ePub 978-1-80424-265-0
PDF 978-1-80424-266-7

Published by MX Publishing
335 Princess Park Manor, Royal Drive, London, N11 3GX
www.mxpublishing.co.uk

Cover design by Brian Belanger

Introduction

To date, the various tales which have made their way from the tin dispatch box, which I won at an estate auction in St. Andrew's, Scotland, to the printed page have included, for the most part, adventures that were at least in part coloured by the politics of the day. *The Vatican Cameos* and *The Stone of Destiny* both had political overtones, and it is easy to understand Dr. Watson's reticence in publishing them.

However, I was not quite prepared for the doings of Holmes and his Boswell in the case which I have taken the liberty of titling *The Devil's Disciples*. For some inexplicable reason, Dr. Watson left this particular exploit untitled – a rarity among the good doctor's papers.

Many Holmesian chronologists will agree that the years 1884 and 1885 are a black hole in the Canon. We can safely place *The Speckled Band* in 1883, but of the 60 stories, none is set in 1884 or 1885. After reading Watson's untitled tale, I think I know why a portion of one of those years has remained a void.

This case certainly posed a challenge to the intrepid duo. I have to believe that the events that transpired and the possibility of those not brought to justice possibly exacting vengeance of some sort certainly must have loomed large in the doctor's mind. So the decision to withhold the story from publication may have been prompted in equal parts by Watson's concern for the safety of those near and dear to Holmes and himself – as well as for their own personal security. There was also Holmes' reticence about the case – which he apparently did not consider one of his crowning achievements and about which it appears he had decidedly mixed emotions.

The tale that follows is a complex adventure that finds Holmes and Watson serving Queen and Country – albeit with varying degrees of success and enthusiasm. While it certainly finds them in unfamiliar territory, it also reveals a great deal about their relationship and their shared values.

Let me stop here, lest I say too much. My only hope is that you enjoy this particular tale – no matter what your political persuasion – as much as I have.

– Richard Ryan

Prologue

Let me begin by quoting Mr. Charles Dickens,

"It was the best of times, it was the worst of times,
it was the age of wisdom, it was the age of foolishness,
it was the epoch of belief, it was the epoch of incredulity,
it was the season of light, it was the season of darkness,
it was the spring of hope, it was the winter of despair."

In the late 1860s and continuing through much of the 1870s, all seemed bright for the future of the Empire. In 1773, in the wake of the territorial acquisition that followed the British victory in the Seven Years' War, George Macartney had written of "this vast empire on which the sun never sets, and whose bounds nature has not yet ascertained." That sentiment was echoed nearly a century later when Alexander Campbell used the phrase to express the dominion of Britain and its vast holdings.

Admittedly things were far from perfect. To be sure, there were wars abroad, but at home all was relatively peaceful until the persistent question of Irish Home Rule once again reared its head in the 1860s with Fenian uprisings both here and in Canada. Frustrated by England's refusal to give ground on even the slightest issue and exacerbated by the actions of such men as Sir Charles Trevelyan during the Great Famine, which plagued Ireland from 1845 until 1849, the Irish, or perhaps I should say some members of the Irish Republican Brotherhood, decided to take matters into their hands. As a result, the first half of the 1880s were marred by fear and terror as the Irish fought back.

Their response to John Bull's obdurate stance was to launch a bombing campaign largely aimed at London and its residents. The objective, I suppose, was to instill such fear in the hearts of the residents of the city that they would pressure members of Parliament to consider giving the Irish their freedom.

Knowing what I now know about the treatment many of the Irish received at the hands of Her Majesty's government and its subjects – and having experienced it myself first-hand to some small degree – I can certainly understand their desire to be rid of their overbearing masters. Still, I cannot condone the actions undertaken during the bombing campaign. After all, the average Londoner had no more to do with the policies of Her Majesty's government than I had to do with ending the second Afghan War.

But I digress. When Holmes was asked to try to bring an end to the reign of terror, he did not hesitate nor did I. Little did we suspect the twisted road upon which we had set out.

For any number of reasons, not the least of which is a request by Holmes himself, I am consigning this story to my tin dispatch box which is kept in the vaults at Cox & Co. in Charing Cross. There is little doubt in my mind that it will ever come before the public. A few of the personages involved are too august and the machinations that were employed to stymie my friend's efforts and thus prolong the bombings are almost Machiavellian in nature.

Still, I refuse to sit here more than a decade later and pass judgment on anyone. People followed their hearts and their consciences – as misguided as they may have been. Now, I am not so blinded by Queen and Country as to fail to see the other side of the coin as clearly as I should. Although that may have been the case once, I do believe it is not so any longer.

If, by some chance, someone should happen to read this letter and the tale that follows, I leave the task of judging to you.

After all, I was there, I was involved, I lived through it; as a result, mine is hardly an unbiased opinion.

– Dr. John H. Watson, MD

14 December, 1896

"Terror is only justice: prompt, severe and inflexible; it is then an emanation of virtue; it is less a distinct principle than a natural consequence of the general principle of democracy, applied to the most pressing wants of the country."

– Maximilien Robespierre

"Oh Liberty, how many crimes are committed in thy name?"

– Madame Roland, while being led to her execution, 1793

"Must I at length the Sword of Justice draw?
Oh curst Effects of necessary Law!
How ill my Fear they by my Mercy scan,
Beware the Fury of a Patient Man."

– John Dryden

Chapter 1 – 14 December, 1884

It was a rare occasion when I arose before my friend, Sherlock Holmes. However, as I had been summoned to my surgery quite early that Sunday due to a medical emergency, I returned home and found myself finishing my breakfast just as Holmes emerged from his bedroom around half seven. Enraged by what I had just read in *The Times*, I exclaimed, "Holmes, they've done it again!"

My friend looked at me in bewilderment and calmly said, "Pray be precise with your pronouns, Watson. Having not yet had the opportunity to peruse the papers, I am totally at sea with regard to whom your 'they' might refer, nor would I even care to hazard a guess as to exactly what 'they' have done, for the 'it' in your sentence is also singularly uninformative."

"The Fenians! The Fenians!" I yelled. "They tried to bomb London Bridge last evening."

"It would seem apparent from your use of the word 'tried' that the attempt was unsuccessful," he offered.

It was the morning of 14 December, 1884, and we were now in the third year of a campaign that had seen members of the Irish Republican Brotherhood, in conjunction with its American counterpart, a group that called itself the *Clan na Gael*, employing bombs as their weapons of choice in a series of attacks that had shown little, if any, discrimination. "That makes at least a dozen attempted bombings in the last three years," I stated.

"I believe the exact number is fourteen attempts – although there may be others of which I am unaware – involving some twenty bombs all told," replied Holmes. "Fortunately, on at least three of the occasions the bombs were either discovered and successfully defused before they could explode, or the timing device malfunctioned in some way thus preventing the bomb's detonation. Now do tell me more about this latest attempt at the bridge."

"According to *The Times,* members of the Irish Republican Brotherhood or sympathizers with their cause were attempting to plant a bomb at one of the piers under the bridge when it appears to have exploded prematurely. Surprisingly, little damage apparently was done to the bridge itself, but windows on both sides of the Thames were blown out, and the bombers' boat was completely destroyed. As a result, the police are uncertain if they somehow managed to escape or if they fell victim to the explosion."

Sipping a cup of coffee, Holmes peered over the rim at me and said, "I should think given the severity of the blast which you have described, any would-be bombers perished as a result. Still, I suppose we shall have to wait until the bodies are recovered – if indeed, they ever are."

As you might expect, the latest atrocity perpetrated by the Fenians was all anyone could talk about for the next few days. Whether at my surgery or at my club, the bombing was on everyone's mind. Judging from the snatches of conversation I picked up from people I passed in the street, Londoners of all stripes were once again feeling unsafe in their own city. More concerning was the fact that I thought I detected a certain unease, and perhaps a growing mistrust of the government.

Things grew even worse a week later, when on December 20, the *Illustrated London News* ran a dramatic full-page drawing on its front page depicting the flash of the explosion beneath the bridge as seen and described by witnesses crossing over the span above. It was a remarkable drawing, but all it did was rub anew the already raw nerves of the average Londoner.

The holiday season was marred further when news spread on Christmas Day that the mutilated remains of one of the bombers had been discovered downriver. Although the body of the other man was never recovered, the police were later able to conclude that the bombing had been the work of two Americans, William Mackey Lomasney and John Fleming.

The bombers were eventually identified because a young man reported to police that he had found dynamite in the bookshop his mother had rented to two American gentlemen who had gone missing after the 13th of December. Apparently he had entered the premises to see if all was well with the two men and to try to collect what was owed when he stumbled across the explosives.

With that bit of information, Scotland Yard was able to piece together who had been behind the attack. As it turned out, the two men had already been under surveillance by the police, both in America and in Britain. There was some speculation a third man might have been involved, but the authorities were never able to say with absolute certainty whether the bombers numbered two or three.

Although 1885 arrived with hope and fanfare, things quickly turned somber when a bomb exploded in a tunnel at the Gower Train Station on the 2nd of January. Fortunately, no one was badly injured, although some passengers were cut by flying shards of glass. Still, the damage had been done, and the capital was on edge once again.

One evening, a few days after the latest atrocity, I asked Holmes why he had not taken more of an interest in the case.

"These Fenian fiends are terrorizing the entire city. You must do something," I pleaded.

He looked at me and then replied rather cryptically, "What makes you think I haven't?" He then resumed his experiments at his chemistry table.

I debated pursuing the issue and then decided against it. At that time, Holmes and I had been friends for only a few years, and although I had assisted on a number of cases, we were still trying to ascertain exactly where we stood with each other. I also knew if Holmes wanted to make me privy to his actions, he would – but only when he was ready.

As you might expect, after a week or so, the train station bombing, like all the others before it, had been replaced with the latest scandals at home and news from abroad. By mid-January, the 17th to be exact, spirits were buoyed when the British scored a resounding victory at the Battle of Abu Klea in the long-running Mahdist War.

However, our joy was short-lived because on the 24th of January, three bombs exploded – one each in the House of Commons chamber, in the banqueting room in the Tower of London, and in Westminster Hall. To make matters worse, just four days later, on the 28th of January, the British-Egyptian forces which had defended Khartoum during a long siege were finally overrun. Virtually the entire garrison was killed, and General Charles Gordon, the commander of the British-Egyptian forces, was beheaded during the attack.

After the triple bombing, I felt certain that Holmes would involve himself in the affair, and I was proven correct when on the morning of the 29th, the bell sounded shortly after nine o'clock. Mrs. Hudson knocked on the door a moment later.

Holmes bade her enter and when she did it was apparent she was a bit flustered.

"Mr. Holmes," she began, "there's a gentleman downstairs asking if he might have a few moments of your time. He seems rather firm about the matter, sir." With that she handed Holmes the man's card. My friend glanced at it and said, "By all means, show him up."

Since Holmes often required privacy when interviewing clients, I rose and started to go to my bedroom. "Stay, Watson," said Holmes, "I think you may want to hear what our visitor has to say. You never know, it may make a fitting subject for one of those tales with which you have been busying yourself of late."

A few minutes later, a dapper young man of perhaps 30, entered our rooms. He was tall and slim and carried himself with a certain gravity. He was quite a striking fellow, but his handsome visage was marred by an obvious unease that was readily discernible in his face. He bowed to Holmes and then me, and said, "Mr. Holmes, I am Robert Orr, first deputy to Assistant Commissioner James Monro."

"Both of your names are well-known to me," replied Holmes.

Orr looked at Holmes and then continued, "I do not normally take such liberties as dropping in on someone unannounced so early in the day, but the situation confronting us is one of such urgency that I am quite willing to forego social niceties if it means we arrive at a resolution sooner rather than later."

"Pray be seated," said Holmes. "Would you care for coffee or tea?"

"Nothing for me," replied Orr.

"You have come about the Fenian bombings?" inquired Holmes.

Taken aback by my friend's directness, our visitor looked first at Holmes and then at me before returning his gaze to Holmes as he sat there in silence.

Finally, Holmes broke the silence. "You may speak freely in front of Dr. Watson," he said, waving his hand in my direction. "He is the epitome of discretion."

I was quite moved by the compliment my friend had just paid me, but I said nothing.

Our guest looked at me and stated, "I trust you understand everything I am about to tell you must remain in the strictest confidence. Lives may well depend on your sense of 'discretion.'"

I nodded and said, "I understand, Mr. Orr."

Our visitor then began to recount in great detail a number of the various outrages perpetrated by the members of the Irish Republican Brotherhood working in concert with members of *Clan na Gael* over the last three years. I watched Holmes carefully, and I could see that on one or two occasions he appeared surprised at what he was being told.

After about fifteen minutes, our visitor concluded, "Thus far, we have been most fortunate. Between our spies in the Brotherhood, paid informers both here and in Ireland America, and sheer ineptitude on the part of the bombers, the damage has been largely confined to property. While many people have been injured – some quite seriously – there have been only three deaths to date."

"Yes, the young boy who perished in January 1881 when the barracks at Salford in Lancashire were targeted, and I presume the other two fatalities would be the Americans who attempted to blow up the London Bridge."

"You have it exactly, Mr. Holmes. I can see that you have given this matter some thought."

"Indeed, I have," replied my friend. "Had you not called here today, you might well have seen me in the offices of Assistant Commissioner Monro later this week where I would have offered my services."

"And trust me, sir, he would have accepted your offer. He was given his position with a mandate that he end the bombings."

"So, what's to be done?"

"As you can see Mr. Holmes, the bombers grow bolder. As I mentioned, last May a bomb exploded at the headquarters of Metropolitan Police Criminal Investigation Department which was aimed at the Special Irish Branch in Scotland Yard. That same night two other bombs exploded – one in the basement of the Carlton Club, a well-known haunt for Conservative MPs; and the other was detonated outside the home of Conservative MP Sir Watkin Williams Wynn."

"I recall it all too well," replied Holmes. "Ten people were injured and I believe a fourth bomb, planted at the foot of Nelson's Column, failed to explode."

"You knew about the fourth bomb? But how? We kept that from the public so as not to frighten the citizenry any more than necessary."

"I have my methods," replied Holmes. "If I am to help you in this matter, you must be forthcoming with all the information you have obtained."

A bit chastised, Orr nodded and then said, "And did you know about the bombs on the ships as well?"

"I assume you are referring to the disguised explosives discovered back in 1881 aboard the SS Malta and the SS Bavaria which were berthed in Liverpool."

"Again, you hit the mark."

"I have taken a special interest in these bombings for reasons of my own, but I place my powers, such as they may be, at your disposal."

"As I've said, Mr. Holmes, we have managed to place spies in their ranks, but their knowledge is limited to their immediate circle. The structure of the group is such that a premium is placed on secrecy. Moreover, the Irish Republican Brotherhood has roots on both sides of the Atlantic as well as in England and Scotland. Making matters worse, there are sections of Ireland where they are seemingly beyond the reach of the law – unless they slip up badly.

"Add to that the vagaries of the government where Mr. Gascoyne-Cecil and Mr. Disraeli seem to be constantly vying with each other for the position of Prime Minister and any political solution to the problem will not soon be forthcoming."

"What is it you would like me to do?" asked Holmes.

"Somehow, you must find a way to end this reign of terror. Tensions between native Englishmen and the Irish who have emigrated here after the potato famine have always been strained, but these senseless bombings have brought things to a boil. Lately it appears as though anyone who speaks with even a hint of a brogue is looked upon with suspicion, and heaven help the poor Irishman seen walking through the streets carrying a bag."

"I will certainly give the matter some thought," replied Holmes. "Hopefully, I will be able to devise a plan to capture the dynamiters so that people may sleep in their beds without fear of their neighbors and what the next day may bring."

"It is imperative that you do so, Mr. Holmes. One of the men we have inserted into one of the groups has alerted us to the fact that they are expecting a new, and if he is to be believed, far more proficient bomb-maker."

"That was to be expected," said Holmes, "as these groups evolve, they also advance in terms of the methods they employ. Also, they needed to replace the men lost in the London Bridge bombing, and their efforts since then have been woefully ineffective, fortunately."

"That's true, Mr. Holmes. However, he has also informed us they plan to step up the campaign by detonating multiple bombs on a daily basis until Ireland is given its freedom."

The discussion continued for several more minutes before Orr took his leave. I walked him to the door, and when I turned around I saw Holmes heading towards his bedroom.

"I say, Holmes, what are you doing?"

"I'm going to work," he replied before he vanished into his bedroom and pushed the door closed behind him.

Chapter 2

I stood there dumbfounded. Holmes' words had stung me – "I'm going to work." My friend had just been tasked with ending the bombing campaign that had been terrorizing the citizens of London for more than three years, and it appeared as though I were to play little or no role in what I considered to be our most important case to date.

Some 20 minutes later Holmes emerged from his room, walking with a wooden crutch and dragging his left leg behind him. As you might expect, the transformation was incredible. Having donned clothing that seemed more rags than garments, Holmes had also blackened his teeth, face, and hands and he now stood there leaning on his crutch. Atop his head was a worn woolen watch cap. Somehow in a short time he had transformed himself into perhaps the most pitiable pauper in all of London.

Forgetting my hurt feelings, I couldn't help but exclaim, "My word, Holmes, that is extraordinary."

"Nothin' so grand as t'at," he replied in a thick brogue. "Just rahquires practice, 'tis all." As he headed for the door, he stopped and turned back. My face must have given me away. For suddenly, he stood erect, looked at me and said, "Much is expected of us, Doctor. Only right now, it is my time. Do not fret, old friend. Yours will come." Then slipping back into character, he added, "Don' wait up. I may be away fer a few days."

I saw nothing of Holmes for the next three days, and when he finally reappeared late in the afternoon on the 1st of February, he looked even more wretched and bedraggled than he had when he had departed. During our time together, I had learned it was best to let him tell his tale in his own time and manner.

Having thrown himself into his chair, still wearing his rags, he charged his pipe, lit it with an ember from the hearth and sat there smoking in silence for several minutes. Finally, he looked at me, smiled apologetically, and said, "This may be the most difficult challenge we have ever encountered, old friend. It will certainly be one of the most perilous."

Taking a moment to reflect on the successes we had enjoyed, I replied with a remark that I look back on and at which I now wince. "I should think by now we are well-acquainted with danger." At that point, I was filled with the infallibility of a man in his prime, but I realize now my reply was tinged as much by confidence as by hubris.

When Holmes didn't reply immediately, I continued, "Given the stakes, I am certain it will prove daunting, but difficult? For you?"

"The Irish in London are a tight-knit group. They do not take kindly to strangers – even those who claim to hail from Donegal – and given the treatment they have received, I can certainly understand their antipathy towards all things British.

"Infiltrating their secret societies is going to be a long and arduous process. It will certainly take weeks at a minimum, perhaps even months."

"And while you are …"

"Not me, Watson, rather we. If you recall, I did tell you your time would come."

"If they abhor all things British, how can I be of assistance? You are the actor, my friend. I am not nearly so deft at dissembling as you are."

"I'm going to take that as a compliment, old friend," he said, smiling. "However, I am going to require your assistance. As for your acting ability, or lack thereof, I believe I have devised a solution."

"I hope it will explain away my British accent and mannerisms. Holmes, if you can transform this old soldier into a son of the auld sod," I said in my best Irish accent, "more's the credit to you."

Holmes chuckled, but as you might have expected, he had planned carefully. He said dryly, "I know you are as British as John Bull, but there are Watsons scattered throughout Ireland, especially in the northern sections of that country. According to my research, there is a particularly strong contingent of Watsons to be found in the province of Ulster, centered in and around County Antrim. Although the area is primarily Protestant, there are communities of Catholics in Ulster, but they are definitely in the minority."

"Well, that's all well and good, but I don't think my brogue will fool any self-respecting son of Eire."

"Sadly, you are correct in that respect," Holmes said smiling. "However, if your parents had fled their homeland in 1850, and you were born two years later in England, that would account for your proper British accent. Also, it might help considerably if you could eschew proper speech for the foreseeable future and attempt to employ a bit more street patois in your vocabulary."

Although Holmes relished playing "dress-up" as I called it, and I loathed it, this was a case where I had to ignore my feelings and put Queen and Country first.

"What would you have me do, Holmes?"

"First, I am going to conduct some research into the Irish in Whitechapel and Spitalfields and see if we can't find some distant relatives of yours living there."

"What about you? Do you have 'distant relatives' in Whitechapel as well?"

"I believe I have a number of cousins there who will attest to my heritage, if need be, and, if things go well, in a few more weeks, you'll have several cousins as well, and perhaps even a niece or nephew, vouching for you to boot.

"Now, if you really want to be of service, spend the next week in the British Library reading anything and everything that pertains to recent Irish history. You'll have to be convincing and part of being convincing is knowing what you are talking about. You must study for this as though you were preparing for a part in a play; unfortunately, this is all too real and there is no room for error."

"I shall do my best, Holmes."

"I know that, my friend. However, there is one more thing I must tell you."

"Out with it, man."

"As I have indicated, I believe this may prove to be a rather lengthy investigation."

"Yes, I rather imagined that it would be."

"Indeed, to that end, I think it best that we move out of Baker Street – at least temporarily."

"What? Where will we live? What about our rooms here?"

"We are keeping the rooms here. After all, we will need a place to call home when this is over."

"But where will we be living?"

"As you are aware, I keep several hidey-holes throughout London, one of which is in Whitechapel, but I think for the foreseeable future, we shall be calling one or more of the doss houses in that area our home."

"A doss house? You can't be serious. Can't we just sneak back here at night?"

"And if we were followed, the game would be up, and one can only wonder what these bombers might do to 221B. No, Watson, we must live our parts – not merely play them."

And that was when the reality hit me: It was not just our lives that hung in the balance. If these fiends escaped, no one in London would be safe.

Steeling myself, I put on a brave face, looked at Holmes and said, "What time does the library open?"

Holmes merely smiled at me and said, "Good old, Watson."

Chapter 3

I must say my first visit to the library was an eye-opening experience. I had no idea that Arthur Wellesley, the Duke of Wellington and hero of the Battle of Waterloo, had played such a prominent role in having King George IV sign the Roman Catholic Relief Act of 1829. Perhaps more popular than the King at the time, Wellington had threatened to resign from his position as Prime Minister unless His Majesty signed the act into law. I should have loved to have been a party to those conversations – especially since Wellington had been born and raised in the Anglican faith.

On I read and I must admit the English treatment of the Irish especially under people such as Sir Charles Trevelyan was at best inhumane. Trevelyan's response to the potato blight may have directly resulted in the death of thousands, perhaps hundreds of thousands, of Irish because as he wrote "the judgement [sic] of God sent the calamity to teach the Irish a lesson." Seeing God's hand in the misery and deaths of hundreds of thousands and the displacement of millions more, struck me as unconscionable.

After several hours I had gained a certain superficial familiarity with events in Irish history since the turn of the century. I returned home that evening to find Holmes rummaging through his yearbooks. I related my day to him, and said, "While I can certainly understand the resentment, I still cannot condone a campaign that targets innocent civilians."

After listening to my objections, Holmes responded, "I'm inclined to agree with you, Watson. There are better ways to get your point across, but that is the path they have chosen, and it has fallen to us to end this campaign."

While we were speaking, Mrs. Hudson knocked on the door, and Holmes bade her enter. "Dinner, such as it is, is served, gentlemen," she announced. With that, she placed two covered dishes on the table which had already been set.

As she departed, Holmes said, "I trust everything has been prepared as I instructed."

"Yes, sir," she replied. As she walked past me towards the door, she rolled her eyes. I didn't grasp the meaning of that action immediately.

"What an odd remark," I thought to myself, pondering its significance.

The meaning soon hit me as I lifted the cover from my platter and saw two small boiled potatoes, a few leaves of steamed cabbage and a small piece of meat, which I assumed was pork of some sort. "Holmes? What is the meaning of this?"

Holmes chuckled as he explained, "With all due respect, Doctor, we are going to attempt to blend in with people who are living in abject poverty and getting by on perhaps one decent meal a day – if that. By contrast, you are the picture of health. I am afraid that for you to insinuate yourself into the Irish enclaves, you are going to have to sport the 'lean and hungry look' which the Bard mentions in *Julius Caesar*. To that end, I'd suggest that you lose at least one stone, perhaps a bit more if possible, avoid your barber for the foreseeable future, and perhaps grow your beard to complement your moustache."

I suddenly realized how Holmes was able to submerge himself into the characters he assumed. He became them! "I shall do my best, Holmes."

"That's all I can ask, old friend."

I knew it wasn't going to be easy, but I kept reminding myself of the stakes. As you might expect, dinner was brief as there wasn't much to eat. After we had taken our seats in front of the fireplace, I considered pouring myself a brandy, but when I looked to the sideboard, I realized all the decanters had been emptied and the gasogene was missing.

"I thought it best to remove all forms of temptation," said Holmes placidly.

"When this is over …"

Holmes cut me off exclaiming, "We will enjoy a grand dinner at either Rules or Simpson's, my treat and your choice."

"No expense spared?"

"None!"

"Done," I exclaimed.

As I was about to light my cigar, Holmes said, "There is one more thing…"

"And what might that be?"

"I'd suggest you enjoy that cigar and then tomorrow you can start practicing rolling your own cigarettes."

"You don't mean?"

"I'm afraid I do. We will be living in near poverty; as a result, luxuries such as brandy, cigars and packets of cigarettes will be well beyond our means."

Recalling the image of Holmes attired in rags, I asked, "And I suppose we must dress the part as well."

"We must, I'm afraid. We are creating an illusion and anything that rings false could have terrible consequences for us as well as the Empire."

Suddenly a new thought hit me. "Holmes, how will you explain our absence to Mrs. Hudson?"

Reaching into his pocket, he produced two tickets, "I have told her the truth – or at least as much as she needs to know. Should anyone ask, she will simply say that we have gone to America," he exclaimed. "As a matter of fact, I have booked passage for us on the Cunard liner RMS Scythia. She sails from Liverpool in a fortnight. We shan't be on it, of course, but we will take the train from Euston north. However, we will disembark long before Liverpool, change out attire and make our way back to London, unbeknownst to anyone."

"And why, pray tell, are we going to America?"

"You can let it be known that Mr. Allan Pinkerton has requested my assistance in a case of some significance."

"I didn't know you knew Pinkerton."

"I've never met the man but we have corresponded on a number of occasions, and he has agreed to vouch for my story."

"Does he know what you are actually doing?"

"No, but he has agreed to help me anyway."

"And what about Scotland Yard? Will you tell Lestrade or Gregson? Surely, you will make them privy to our plans."

"I think not – at least initially. The fewer people who know, the less chance there is of a slip." Having made that pronouncement, Holmes looked at me, smiled, and said, "I do hope you are relishing that cigar."

The next ten days were monotonous. I saw patients in the morning and remained in the library until closing time, reading about the exploits of Daniel O'Connell, who in 1829 became the first Catholic member of Parliament since 1659; the Tithe War of the 1830s, in which the English tried to get Catholics to pay for the maintenance of the Protestant Church; the Great Famine and the mass emigration that followed; all of which seemed to culminate in the formation of the Home Rule League, which became the Irish Parliamentary Party and the sudden rise to fame of young Charles Stewart Parnell.

However, interesting as those articles may have been, I found myself absolutely fascinated by the reports detailing the activities of the Irish Republican Brotherhood. Much to my surprise, I learned that their first bombing had taken place in 1862 when an attempt was made to free one of the members from prison. Twelve people were killed in the blast which served only to destroy a significant portion of the prison wall.

Just a few years ago, in 1882, a breakaway branch calling itself the Irish National Invincibles, had assassinated the British Chief Secretary for Ireland, Lord Frederick Cavendish and Thomas Henry Burke, the permanent undersecretary at the Irish office. Both men were stabbed to death only hours after Cavendish had arrived in Dublin in what became known as the Phoenix Park Murders. It eventually came out at trial that Burke had been the principal target and Cavendish was killed because he happened to be walking with Burke. "These are treacherous waters, indeed," I thought.

The day before we were ready to depart for Liverpool, Holmes quizzed me over dinner, such as it was. Much to his surprise and my own, I was able to answer all of his questions. When he had finished, he exclaimed, "Well done, Hamish."

23

"Hamish?"

"Yes, I think it best you go by your middle name. After all, there's no telling how popular your stories are among the working class."

"And what shall I call you? Surely Sherlock is too well-known to use as a *nom de guerre.*"

"I shall be going by the name Fergus."

"Interesting choice," I remarked.

"Now do get used to it, for once we step out the door tomorrow morning, those are our names. One slip and we might well be undone.

"I assume you are all packed?"

I nodded.

"Excellent, Mrs. Hudson will serve breakfast at half six, and then we are off."

I decided to turn in early and as I ascended the stairs to my room, I turned back and said, "Good night, Fergus."

I slept surprisingly well and was already dressing when Holmes yelled up, "Breakfast is served."

Despite Holmes' objections, Mrs. Hudson had prepared a full English breakfast, and having slightly more than a stone in the past two weeks, I savoured each bite, for I knew I should not see food like this for some time to come.

We thanked Mrs. Hudson for the meal, I somewhat more profusely than Holmes. We then bade her farewell and hailed a cab for Euston. We each carried a battered Gladstone bag, which Holmes had procured, and we caught the 8:10 train to Liverpool.

While we were waiting, I bought a newspaper and learned that dynamite had been discovered the previous evening on Harrow Road. When I showed the article to Holmes, he remarked only, "I suspect their new bomb-maker has not yet arrived, and if he has, he seems even less talented than his predecessors."

The train ride was spent in silence and perhaps three hours later, we disembarked at Rugby. Although the waiting room was fairly empty, we changed from our traveling clothes into our rags in a nearby woods.

Holmes then brought both bags to the station where he told the stationmaster a man had given him a pound to make certain the bags were shipped to Euston and held there to be called for. Having done that, we started walking back towards London. Had I known what awaited us, I might well have remained in Rugby.

We made it about a third of the way back to London that first day, thanks to a farmer who gave us a ride for about 20 miles. We slept rough outside the village of Bletchley. The next day was more of the same, and finally the following evening after walking most of the way, we arrived back in London around eight.

We made our way to Spitalfields where we procured four-penny coffin beds at a doss house on Flower and Dean Street. I thought I had seen humanity at its lowest level, but nothing had prepared me for the abject poverty of that room. Hundreds of narrow wooden boxes sat next to each other on the floor. People of all ages were jammed into a single room, and they were treated worse than cattle. Our four pence had bought us the right to sleep in one of those "beds." There was a communal kitchen and the other facilities were equally lacking. As a result the place was permeated by an odour which was impossible to escape and which I know I shall never forget.

Although Holmes had tried to prepare me for the doss house, there are no words capable of doing that dreadful place justice.

As you can imagine, I slept little during our stay there. However, Holmes appeared to be familiar with a number of the denizens of this particular establishment. As he renewed acquaintanceships, he would introduce me as his friend, Hamish, and say we had been forced to lie low. "No one's been looking for me, have they?" he would ask, and then he would spin a tale about where he had been.

We spent nearly a fortnight in that wretched place, and seeing the children forced to live there broke my heart. Given what I saw transpire in that room, it might as well have been a school for the next generation of English ne'er-do-wells and drabs. Still, each day we would rise early and walk to St. Katherine Docks where we would look for work, earning between three and five shillings a day. It was hard, back-breaking labour, but Holmes was cultivating an array of new friends. Occasionally, we were turned away because of Holmes' brogue, but more often than not we were able to find work. After a grueling day, we would stop at a few pubs and before long, we were recognized by most of the publicans.

Always in character, Holmes would occasionally stand some of our co-workers to a pint and he would always offer the traditional Irish toast, "Sláinte," which our companions would reciprocate with gusto. So convincing was Holmes as an amiable Irishman that had I not known it was my friend, I might have thought I was standing next to someone from Donegal.

Chapter 4

After two weeks in the miserable doss house, Holmes let it be known that we had "saved" enough to take a small room in Whitechapel. Located on Weyhill Road, a narrow thoroughfare that runs the short distance from Commercial Road to Coke Street, our flat was actually Holmes' bolt-hole in that section of the city. Small and spartan, the room featured two cots, an uneven table with three chairs, two stools, a fireplace, a few dishes, cups and glasses and little else. The walls and ceiling were cracked plaster and at some point in the distant past, an effort had been made to whitewash them. However, smoke from the hearth and time had long since turned the white into a dingy grey.

Holmes seemed aloof to the dismal surroundings, saying by way of explanation, "I normally keep makeup and various disguises here, but I cleared all that out a few weeks ago in anticipation of our prolonged stay."

I didn't care where I was residing so long as I was out of the doss house and away from those four-penny coffin beds.

"How about your neighbors? Aren't they suspicious of the fact that you are never here?"

"There are two sisters – Jenny and Julie – who live across the hall. They are charming young women, and I've led them to believe I'm a sailor when I can get work, so there's no need to explain my prolonged absences; they think I'm at sea. As for the rest of the tenants, I am as invisible to them as they are to me.

"I chose this flat as much for its location as the fact there is a back alley that takes me out to Coke Street. I can come in the front door in disguise and exit through the back as myself with no one the wiser.

"Now, Watson, I think it's time for lunch and to meet some of the other denizens of Whitechapel. What say you to a meat pie and a tankard of ale at the Ten Bells?"

Located on the corner of Commercial and Fournier streets in Spitalfields, the Ten Bells was not at all what I had expected. The interior featured a great deal of dark wood. The walls were tiled and quite handsome, and the pub might have been at home in any number of the more well-to-do sections of London. Two of the walls featured a blue floral pattern which was highlighted by a tile dado running around the entire room.

Holmes and I ordered two tankards of ale and meat pies and sat at a small table by the window. Holmes had nodded to and exchanged pleasantries with several people when we arrived, including the barman. On one side was a table of what I guessed were German workers while at another table on the other side of the room, three or four Irishmen had gathered. There were one or two ladies sitting at the bar, but the word "ladies" might be a bit misleading in their case.

We sat there conversing in a low tone of voice when all of a sudden one of the Irishmen said loud enough for us to hear, "I'm telling you there's no other way. It's the only thing these people understand."

My ears perked up, but Holmes either hadn't, or pretended not to have, heard.

"Easy there, Seamus," one of the men remarked. "Sayin' stuff like t'at won't do anyone any good."

"How can you say that to me, Donal? After all, didn't your Da lose his farm to one of the absentee British blighters?"

"T'at he did, but I'm livin' here now. Me and ta family are gettin' on and everyone's a whole lot less hungry than they were back then."

"You're getting' soft, Donal."

"No, Seamus, I'm just being clever. Do I wish t'ings was better? Absolutely! Will I work to change the present situation? Of course! But I draw the line at indiscriminate killin'."

At that point, I glanced over and one of the fellows sitting there happened to take notice of me. He nudged the fellow next to him, whispered something and then they both stood up and came over to our table.

"It's rude to eavesdrop," said one. "Didn't your ma teach you no manners?"

"You're quite right," replied Holmes. "But it's also stupid to have a conversation like that in a public place where you can be easily overheard. S'pose we was coppers?"

At that they both laughed, although the one called Seamus managed to sneak a glance at his surroundings before he joined his companion.

"You must be new here or you'd know that coppers are few and far between in Whitechapel and Spitalfields," said Donal.

"We are relatively new here," replied Holmes, "just in from Liverpool."

"And what brings you to this fair city?" asked Seamus.

"We needed to leave Liverpool in a bit of a hurry, if you catch my drift. And that's all I'll be sayin' 'bout that."

"Oh, it's like t'at, is it?" asked Donal. "Well, if you're lookin' to 'ide out from the peelers, you've come to the right spot."

Holmes then signaled to the waiter, "A round for my friends here."

"Thank'ee," said Donal. "Won't you join us?"

"Not today," replied Holmes. "I 'ave t'ings t'at need attendin' to. Perhaps next time."

After paying the bill, we left the Ten Bells and headed back to our flat. Knowing better than to discuss such matters in public, I remained silent. When we entered our building, I saw the sisters, Jenny and Julie, and waved to them before we entered our room. They were dark-haired young ladies, a few years apart in age, with an air of determination about them.

"I don't understand," I said with just a hint of exasperation in my voice. "Those men just invited us to join them. Who knows what we might have learned."

"I can assure you, old friend, we would have learned nothing of significance. Trust has to be earned. We took a small step in that direction today, but had we pressed our luck, I cannot say how things might have turned out."

"Well, I still think we might have learned something."

"We are playing the long game, Watson. We don't want to barge our way into their little group. We want to be invited to join."

"And I suppose you have a plan to accomplish that?"

Holmes smiled enigmatically, "I should think you know me well enough by now to understand that I have several schemes that will ingratiate us with our Irish friends – it's merely a matter of seeing how things progress and then selecting the right one."

Over the next few weeks, we became fairly well-known at a number of the area pubs including The White Hart on Whitechapel High Street, The Brown Bear on Leman Street, and The Castle on Commercial Road. As you might expect, the pubs were frequented by large numbers of labourers of all nationalities although Holmes and I always seemed to find ourselves near or a part of the Irish contingent in whatever public house we managed to end up in.

One morning, Holmes disappeared for the entire day. He told me to tell anyone who asked for him that he had gone to a funeral. We had arranged to meet at seven that evening at The Brown Bear. When I arrived, I could not locate Holmes, so I sat at a table by the window. The pub was fairly crowded, and as you might expect, there were several men with brogues at the bar. Suddenly, Holmes rushed in, ran to the bar, spoke with one of the men, handed him something and then joined me at the table.

Two minutes later two constables entered the pub. After looking around, they set their sights on Holmes. "You there, come here," said one of the officers.

"Can't you see I'm busy," my friend replied.

"Doin' what?"

"I'm waitin' for me pint, what's it look like I'm doin'?" At that all the patrons in the pub began to laugh, and the bobby became even more angry.

"Stand up," the constable ordered, "and turn out yer pockets."

Grumbling under his breath, Holmes stood up and put everything in his pockets on the table.

"Where is it?" the constable asked.

"Wher's wat? You can see everything I have. Unless, of course, you'd like to search me. If you do, promise you'll be gentle," he said mockingly.

At that, the patrons laughed again and hooted and hollered. Shaking his fist in Holmes' face, the constable said, "I know you had something. Just be careful, mister, I've got my eye on you."

With that the constables left the pub. At their departure, the place erupted in applause. Holmes stood, turned to the appreciative audience and took a mock bow. After a few minutes, my friend made his way back to the bar. En route he was greeted by claps on the back and expressions of admiration. Once he had reached the counter, he retrieved what he had given the man when he first entered. He also ordered a round of drinks for the fellow and his companions.

Knowing better than to ask questions, I sat with Holmes as he basked in the adulation of the other pub-goers. It was only when we were back in our room that I asked what had happened. With that he produced what appeared to be a cardboard tube, perhaps eight inches long. "Is that what I think it is?"

"That all depends upon what you think it is," replied Holmes.

Controlling my anger at his flippancy, I said through my teeth, "Dynamite? Is that a stick of dynamite?"

"I'll admit it certainly looks like one, but it's lacking a key ingredient – nitroglycerine. In every other respect from the blasting cap to the *kieselguhr,* or what we call diatomaceous earth, it is a stick of dynamite but in its present state, it is inert and totally harmless."

"What are you going to do with it?"

"With any luck, I'm going to bait a trap. Once word gets out – and it surely will – that I am in possession of and possibly able to procure dynamite, I shouldn't be surprised if our bombers come looking for me."

"And if they don't?"

"Then I shall have to develop another plan, but I am fairly confident that this ruse will succeed."

For the next few days, we kept a low profile. We rose early, went to work, and then returned to the flat. It was a dull, monotonous existence, and I was beginning to have my doubts about Holmes' plan.

One afternoon when we returned home, we met the sisters in the hall. Jenny, who was quite agitated, informed us, "Some men were here looking for you this afternoon."

"Oh?" Holmes replied.

"I can't be certain," Julie added, "but I think they broke into your room."

"Did you see them leave?" asked Holmes.

"There were three of them," Julie said, "and I saw all three leave about an hour ago."

Holmes thanked the young women and gave each a sovereign. "Please have a nice dinner tonight, and thank you for keeping an eye out for me."

As they went into their flat, I said to Holmes, "It's like having a brace of Irregulars living next door."

He smiled and said, "They have been most helpful. If this case weren't so fraught with danger, I'd certainly find more for them to do. They are competent and discreet – two qualities I greatly admire."

Very gingerly, Holmes opened the door a few inches and then dropped to his knees. He then reached inside and I wondered what he was doing since we had been told the men were gone. He then rose and entered, and I followed him in and looked around. At first glance, everything seemed normal enough, and nothing appeared out of place.

"I think the girls may have been mistaken. Everything seems to be just as we left it this morning, and nothing appears to have been taken – not that there is much to take."

"No, the girls were right. Someone has been in this room. Although they covered their tracks, it was immediately obvious to me that the flat has been searched."

"How can you be so sure?"

"Who is the last one out every morning and the first one in every evening?"

"You are. Why? What difference does that make?"

Holmes pointed to the corner where a battered cricket bat stood and a few feet away was a cricket ball.

"Every morning, the last thing I do is reach in and place that ball against the door. When I come home, I always open the door carefully and reach in. If the ball has not moved, no one has entered. When I checked just now, I couldn't reach the ball because it had rolled all the way over to the corner. Someone opened the door causing the ball to move. The bat is there to make it look as though that's where it belongs."

"That's marvelous, Holmes. "

"Simplicity itself."

With that Holmes headed for the fireplace where he examined the box that held the cord wood. Removing all the wood, he reached inside the box and began to count. When he had finished, he announced, "One's missing."

"What is missing?"

"One of the sticks of dynamite I had concealed in that box."

Chapter 5

"You had dynamite here? In this flat? What on Earth for?"

"I should think it would be obvious. We are searching for dynamiters, and I know that explosives can be difficult to procure. In fact, I have it on good authority that some of the Fenians have resorted to making it themselves – and again I have this on good authority – with decidedly mixed results."

"I hope the dynamite was not real. I hope you had rendered it inert just as you did with that other stick?"

Holmes ignored my question, and at that point I realized I had been living just a few feet away from live explosives.

"So what was the point of that whole charade in the pub a few days ago?"

"It was a necessary one, I assure you. I needed word to get about that I could get my hands on dynamite. Of course, the news had to come from someone they trusted."

"In that case, I'm surprised it took them this long."

"I'm not. You see we have been carefully watched for the past three days. I'm sure they were taking note of our schedule. Today, we followed our routine and stopped at The Castle for a pint after work. I'm certain that the reason we were stood to a second round by Jimmy was so that his confederates could search our flat without fear of being disturbed."

"But if they need dynamite, why take only one stick? Why not grab them all?"

"I suspect they hoped that I wouldn't notice the loss of a single stick. After all, I have more than a dozen. However, I'd certainly know if they all went missing."

"Where were you keeping them?"

"The wood box has a false bottom. I also drizzled a bit of oil on the floor."

"Oil? To what end?"

"When dynamite gets old, it can actually leak nitroglycerine in a process known as 'weeping.' Over time, the liquid will pool in the bottom of wherever it is stored. I was hoping they would see the oil stain on the floor next to the box, examine it and discover the false bottom, which is exactly what they did."

A thought struck me, "Holmes, the dynamite they stole could be used in a bombing."

"While there is certainly a chance you may be right, I'm inclined to disagree."

"Why do you say that?"

"I should think they would test any dynamite to make certain of its potency. There's no point in planning a bombing and putting people at risk as they place the explosive – unless you are certain the explosives will do what they are supposed to."

"There is a certain logic to what you say."

"Of course there is," he said smiling.

"So what's the plan?"

"After dark, I want you to put on my coat and hat. Make certain you turn the collar up and pull the brim down low to conceal your face. Then I want you to stick to the best lit streets you can – walk in the middle of the road if you must – and make your way to The Ten Bells. I will join you there later."

"What will you be doing?"

"Hiding the rest of the dynamite in a safe location. There is no point in keeping it here as it has served its purpose. There's also the possibility that whoever took it, once they have tested it, may decide to return for the rest. No, Watson, I have to put it someplace else."

"So I'm to be the distraction?"

"Although I can do a great many things, I haven't yet mastered the art of being in two places at once. Still, you may rest assured that I am working on it."

At about seven that evening, Holmes left the flat carrying a small satchel that I knew contained the dynamite. He went out through the door to Coke Street. About an hour later, wearing Holmes' cap and coat, I left the flat and walked down Weyhill Road, which was a short distance but totally unnerving as there were no streetlamps. The weather was quite brisk and I suddenly took notice of how many streetlamps had been broken and not repaired. The thought did little to comfort me.

I felt much more at ease when I turned onto Commercial Street. Despite the chill, there were a fair number of people out, including a number of ladies offering companionship. As a result, I was able to avoid walking in the street. As I neared Fournier Street, my relief was almost palpable. However it was short-lived as a trio of men came out of Brushfield Street and blocked my way.

Just another fifty feet to safety, I thought. I considered trying to outrun them, but two of them were much younger than I, and the cold wasn't doing my old war wound any favours.

"A word, mate," one of them said.

Discretion being the better part of valour, I replied, "Certainly, what can I do fer ya?"

"T'at's not 'im," one said, and I recognized the man to whom Holmes had handed the dynamite in the pub. I believe his name was Tommy.

"Where's your mate? The tall, thin one," he asked.

Before I could answer, Holmes suddenly appeared behind them and said, "I believe you gents are lookin' for me. What can I do fer ya?"

They quickly recovered from their surprise, and one said, "We need to talk."

Holmes replied, "Talk is cheap, but it takes money to buy whiskey. If you chaps are buyin', I might be persuaded to listen."

"Fine," said the obvious leader. "Let's go to the Ten Bells."

We walked the short distance to the pub and made our way to a corner table in the back. Holmes took a seat so that his back was to the wall. When the waitress approached, the leader held up a hand with his fingers splayed, indicating he wanted five glasses. I noticed that the top halves of two of his fingers were missing. He followed my gaze and laughed, "Dynamite can certainly bite ya if'n yer not careful." At that he burst into laughter as did his two companions.

Holding up his own hands, Holmes remarked, "Obviously, I've been a bit more careful than you." That elicited another round of laughter from the three.

After the whiskey had been served, the third man who had remained silent, said, "I'm Jimmy."

Holmes replied, "I'm Fergus, and this is my friend, Hamish."

"Where are your people from?" asked Jimmy.

"If I had to guess I'd say Galway, but I'd just be guessin'," Holmes replied.

"What do you mean?" demanded one of the men.

"Truth be told, I have no idea who my people are, much less where they're from," replied Holmes. "I was abandoned as an infant and grew up in the Portumna Workhouse. As soon as I was able, I set out on my own, and I've never looked backed?"

"And you, Hamish? Where might ye be from?"

"My family fled Ulster during the famine. My parents left shortly after the blight started and moved to Liverpool, and that's where I was born and spent the first part of my childhood. They've since passed."

"You sound more London than Liverpool," said one.

"We moved here when I was but a wee lad, maybe two or three."

"That explains it then."

"And where did you two meet?" asked another.

"On the docks," Holmes said. "I was havin' a tough time with some British fellas who didn't appreciate my accent. I was holdin' me own against the three of 'em when Hamish stepped in and turned the tide. We've been mates ever since."

"And what, pray tell, is a bloke like you doin' wiv dynamite?"

"You might say it fell into me pocket," he laughed. "I was in the hold of a ship when I dropped a box and it broke open. I knew what it was, and I figured there's always a market for such t'ings. So I stuffed as many sticks as I could in me pants, and hid the rest of the box."

"How much more do you 'ave and what do you want for it?"

"Well, I had 15 sticks, but since you've taken one, I have but 14 left."

"Are you accusin' us of stealin'?"

"Not at all. I'm just going to add the price of the missin' stick to the total. By the way, I hope you tested it 'cause it was weepin' a bit."

"If we 'adn't tested it, we wouldn't be here," said the third man, who had spoken little until this point in time. The other two glared at him, and it took him fully a minute to realize his blunder.

"Colm, why don't you go wait outside while we finish our negotiations here?" suggested Jimmy in a firm tone of voice.

Colm rose and glared at us, but obviously Jimmy was not someone to be trifled with.

"Do you know anything about dynamite besides how to steal it?" he asked Holmes.

"Actually, I know a great deal. I worked at the Bradford Colliery in Manchester for a spell. I watched and I learned, and I was fearless. But I hated goin' down into the mines every day, so after I had saved up a bit, I quit and headed south."

At that point we were joined by a new man who appeared to take the place of Colm. "And are you political?" asked the newcomer who sat down without bothering to introduce himself.

"Are you?" replied Holmes evenly.

"Aye, I'm for a free Ireland, and if you spent time in a workhouse, I should think you would be too."

"I'm for a free Ireland," replied Holmes, "but there are different ways to go about it."

"Mark my words, boyo, Gladstone means well. But the laws he passes change nothin'. And there's no tellin' what Gascoyne-Cecil will do should he ever become Prime Minister. No, I'm afraid Ireland'll have to fend fer herself.

"John Bull understands actions – not words. I'm sorry for the innocents, but in every war there are unforeseen casualties on both sides."

"You mean like those fellas w'at tried to blow up the bridge?" I asked.

The nameless man got red in the face, but quickly brought his emotions under control. "They were soldiers – and martyrs – who died in the service of their country and their religion. One might even say they were doin' the Lord's work."

"The papers would disagree," said Holmes. "What was it the *Illustrated London News* called those fellas – 'Fenian fiends' and 'Irish devils,' I believe."

"Sticks and stones," replied the man.

At which point, Jimmy interjected, "We are certainly not fiends nor are we devils. But I did see one of the London rags describe us as 'the devil's disciples.'"

"Enough of that," the newcomer said. "Let's get back to business." Then he looked hard at Holmes. Since he was quite obviously the leader, I took note of him. He was not quite as tall as Holmes, but more powerfully built with a thick neck and broad shoulders. He had a shock of red hair – that hallmark of the Irish – and bright green eyes that were cold rather than merry. In his lapel, he wore a pin depicting a shamrock which I knew was the symbol of Ireland much like the thistle of Scotland, the daffodil for Wales and the rose for England.

"If the London Bridge attack is the best you can do, you need better bombers," said Holmes. "Half your bombs don't work, and those that do are ineffective."

"Don't you worry about our bomb-makers, mister," said the nameless one.

"I suppose you could do better," sneered Jimmy. "Besides," he continued, "help is on the way."

The nameless one shot him a reproving glance which Holmes ignored before saying, "I certainly couldna do worse"

"Perhaps you'd like to join our cause," offered the nameless one.

"If the price is right," replied Holmes, "and I'll show how to make your own dynamite and then I'll teach ya how to use it as well."

"He's not a patriot," said Jimmy, "He's a stinkin' mercenary."

"But a terribly effective one," replied Holmes.

"The proof is in the puddin'," said Jimmy gamely.

"I'll tell you what," said Holmes. "I'll select the target and provide the dynamite. I'll give you instructions on where and how to place the charge."

"I notice you're not takin' any risk," said Jimmy.

"If the first one goes as planned and you are pleased, you can hire me to do the dirty work in the future."

The nameless one spoke, "Let's just say that we accept your proposition, what next?"

"I'll have some reconnoiterin' to do, and then once I've selected a target, I'll have some plannin' to do as well."

"You sound like a very cautious man," said the nameless one.

"You might say that. Given that I'm working with some dangerous materials, some inexperienced dynamiters and a situation that's as uncertain as your timers, I'm sure you'll not be mindin' if I take my time and do it right. After all, I only get paid if you're satisfied."

The two men looked at each other and the nameless one nodded. They then turned to Holmes and he said, "You have yourself a deal, Mr. Fergus. When can we expect to hear from you?"

"Why don't we meet back here one week from tonight at half eight."

"A week?" Jimmy asked. "Why so long?"

"As yer friend just told ya, I'm a very cautious man."

They agreed, albeit a bit reluctantly on Jimmy's part, and as we were leaving, the man who had never introduced himself said, "Fergus, is that your Christian name or your surname."

Speaking directly to the nameless one, Holmes stated, "Since I don't know your name, what say we just leave it at Fergus?" With that we left the pub and headed back towards our flat.

"Aren't you concerned about being followed?" I asked.

"They know where we live, so that's a moot point. No, at the moment I have far more pressing concerns such as what I can allow them to blow up in London while making certain that no one is injured at the same time."

I started to speak, but then I saw he was lost in thought. He does love a conundrum, I reasoned.

Chapter 6

The next few days, I went to the docks as usual and told the foreman that my friend had come down with a terrible case of influenza. When I described the symptoms in grisly detail, with perhaps more than a bit of embellishment, he said he didn't want to see Fergus again until he was hale and healthy.

As for Holmes, each morning he would arise quite early and leave before the watchers. He told me that he would go to another of his bolt-holes where he would assume one of his many disguises and set out to weigh the possibilities for his upcoming bombing. I must admit that I finally began to appreciate fully his talent in that area.

He returned one evening having spent the day as a disreputable rag-and-bone man. His mood was jaunty as he entered the flat.

"Good news?" I inquired.

"I had a short meeting with Robert Orr, and after I explained to him the progress that we have made thus far, he readily agreed to help me with my plan."

I wondered if Holmes had met Orr while disguised, and if he had, I wondered what Orr's reaction might have been. I was sorely tempted to ask but decided to stick to the topic at hand, "Yes, your 'plan.' You've been very close-mouthed about it and while I normally let you tell your story in your own time, I wonder if you might enlighten me – just this once."

"No apologies, Watson. I've been looking all over London for just the right place to bomb – and safely I might add, as I don't want any injuries or loss of innocent life on my conscience. Yet at the same time I need to impress upon these men my skill and cunning."

"And have you found such a place?"

"Indeed, I have and I must admit that it was a difficult decision. I was torn between the Poet's Corner, the gallery at St. Paul's Cathedral and 10 Downing Street."

"Holmes, you can't be serious!"

Ignoring my protest, he continued blithely, "Ultimately, I decided on the Prime Minister's residence."

I stared at him dumbfounded unable to believe that he had determined to bomb the residence of the Prime Minister.

"You see, Watson. That's a situation where I can control the surroundings to a large degree. There are no tourists inside Downing Street as there are almost certain to be at Westminster and St. Paul's. Moreover, a controlled explosion can be made to look far more devastating from the outside than it actually is, and, more importantly, no one will get hurt."

"Will the government cooperate?"

"I should think so. After all, the powers that be want these bombers caught and the threat to the citizens to end as soon as possible."

"What happens after that?"

"With a little bit of luck, we will be recruited by the Brotherhood and thus we can begin to work against them from the inside."

"I don't suppose it ever occurred to you they might have real grievances."

"I am certain they do, but the fact remains, there are right ways and wrong ways they can employ to redress those wrongs. I believe blowing up innocent citizens definitely falls into the latter category."

We continued our discussion long into the night, with both of us playing devil's advocate at various points.

Two days later we returned to the Ten Bells for our meeting. This time just Jimmy and the other man were waiting for us.

"So what grand plan have you dreamed up?" asked Jimmy with just a hint of scorn in his voice.

"Before we go any further, I think it only fair we all know each other. After all, we're now in this together."

The two men looked at each other. Finally, the nameless one broke the silence, "You may call me Michael."

"And your surname?" inquired Holmes.

"When I know yours, Fergus, you'll know mine," he replied evenly.

"Fair enough," said Holmes, "now let's get down to business." Looking around to make certain that no one was within earshot, Holmes lowered his voice and said, "You want this event to make a statement, am I right on t'at account?"

Both men nodded energetically. "That's the whole point of the campaign. We need to draw attention to the problem," said Michael.

"Well, what would you say, if an event were to take place at Downing Street? Do ya t'ink that would shine the light on your cause?"

"You're mad," exclaimed Jimmy. "You couldn't do that if you wanted to."

"I can and I will, if the price is right. And do you know why I can, Jimmy? Because I possess somethin' you so obviously lack – imagination."

"If you can do that," Michael broke in, "you will have struck a telling blow for Irish freedom. However, since you're not doin' this out of the kindness of your heart, how much?"

Holmes looked at him, appeared to think it over, and then replied, "Freedom always comes at a price and my price is £100. If you're satisfied with the job and if there's more work to be had, I suppose I could be persuaded to lower my rates in the future."

"For £100, you should be doin' the job yaself, and not placin' any of my men at risk," Michael countered.

"I'll be happy to do the job myself, but that will cost you an extra £25."

Michael laughed, "You are a bold one, Mr. Fergus. So I'm going to accept your offer. You'll get half now and the rest when the job is done. I should warn you if you try to cut and run with our money, we will hunt you down and your death will be long and agonizing. So, do we have an understanding?"

"Done," replied Holmes, and he and Michael shook hands.

"One more thing – one of my men will accompany you when you go, and your friend, Hamish, will stay with us until you return."

I expected Holmes to object, but before I could say anything, he replied again, "T'at's a grand idea. In fact, why don't you send that bomb-maker Jimmy mentioned at our last meeting? Perhaps I can show him a thing or two."

"You just worry about making good on your promise," Michael cautioned. "If you decide to join us, I may take you up on your offer if I think it's necessary. Until then, you're nothing more than a hired hand. I trust I have made myself clear."

"Perfectly," said Holmes. "Now about the down payment?"

"I'll meet you here in two days with your money, and I'll be expectin' a rather detailed plan from you."

"T'at won't be a problem," said Holmes, who added, "I'll be here at three in the afternoon."

Everyone seemed taken aback by this statement.

"You're not goin' to do it in broad daylight, are you?" asked Jimmy.

"You'll know everything you need to know in two days' time," said Holmes.

As we were putting on our coats, Michael leaned over and said, "Can you get your hands on any more dynamite? Or would you be willin' to sell us the remaining sticks you 'ave? I'll pay a fair price for it."

"Would that I could," said Holmes. "I'll be requirin' a few sticks for this job, and you never can tell when a sudden need might arise. However, I'll keep my eyes open."

We walked back to the flat in silence. When we were safely inside, Holmes poured us two brandies and we sat on two backless stools in front of the fire. With the cracked plaster and dim lighting, it was a far cry from Baker Street, but still there was a certain familiarity about the situation. I waited in silence as

Holmes filled his pipe and after tamping and lighting it, he looked at me and said, "We are making progress."

"I do hope your plans work out. After all, I'm to be a sort of hostage while you are out blowing up 10 Downing Street."

"While you are in their company, say little, but listen carefully. Some of the men tend to be braggarts. They may let slip some invaluable piece of information."

"And what will you do with the man they send with you?"

"I'll let him help me, of course. This all has to be very carefully stage-managed. However, if we are successful, we may soon find ourselves welcomed into the inner circle of the Irish Republican Brotherhood."

Over the next two days, I saw very little of my friend. Around noon on the day of the meeting, he came into the flat carrying a satchel. From it he extracted two medium-size blue boxes wrapped in white ribbon which I recognized instantly as having come from Tiffany's in Paris. Holmes placed one of the packages carefully on the table, looked at me and said, "You do recognize it, I see."

"Are you going to place the bomb in one of those?"

As we were talking, Holmes set to work removing the disguise he had donned early that morning and transforming himself from a nonconformist clergyman into a proper gentleman complete with a full beard and side-whiskers.

"In a manner of speaking. There is a bomb in the box closest to you already. I'll try to dissuade them from opening it, but I'm certain they'll want to see the goods."

"Why do you need two boxes?"

"It's all part of the plan."

"What happens if they insist upon examining it?"

"I rather suspect they will. Once they've taken a look and are satisfied, you will remain at the Ten Bells while I will deliver the package to 10 Downing Street."

"You're playing a most dangerous game here, Holmes."

"Yes, but I can see no other way to win their trust."

After going over the plan three more times, checking and double-checking each aspect, we finally set out for the pub.

As we entered the Ten Bells, I saw two men standing outside – almost as if they were on sentry duty. Inside there were only three other patrons in the pub, and I suspected they were all Michael's men. As we entered the back room, I saw Jimmy and Michael waiting for us at our usual table. Looking to my right, I also noticed three more men sitting at another table with their backs to us.

Jimmy looked at us and at Holmes and sneered, "Don't you look like a proper toff!"

"I should 'ope so," replied Holmes, "my appearance is an important aspect of this job."

I must admit that Holmes' attire, with his Astrakhan coat and silk waistcoat, stood in stark contrast to the workmen's clothes worn by the rest of us.

As we took our seats at the table with Michael and Jimmy, Holmes said, "You 'ave something for me?"

Michael handed Holmes a fistful of notes. "And have you got a plan for me?"

"I've got more than that." As he spoke, Holmes reached into the satchel and withdrew the boxes placing them on the table. "I'm going to have this one delivered to 10 Downing Street. The timer is set for half four, so I'd suggest that we get on our way."

Michael spoke, "If you don't mind, I'd like to see the device before you leave."

"Just be careful with the ribbon," cautioned Holmes. "Are your hands clean?"

"Why don't you undo it? You can always retie it, can't you?"

Holmes deftly untied the bow and looking around, he lifted up the top so that Michael could peer inside. "Are you sure that's enough dynamite?"

"For our purposes, I think it's more than enough. Any more and we might bring down the whole building."

"Nothin' wrong with that," said Jimmy.

"Are you satisfied, Michael?"

"Indeed, I am, but how are you going to get it into the Prime Minister's residence? And what's the second box for?"

With that Holmes reached into his jacket pocket and withdrew a small envelope. "I think this will help with the delivery, and the second box is a necessary distraction if you will."

He handed the envelope to Michael who examined it and said only, "Clever, very clever."

"We really must be going," Holmes said. "I have a few things I need to do before the package is delivered. Shall we meet back here at around half five?"

"We'll be waiting, Mr. Fergus."

I spent the next two hours glancing at my watch every few minutes. Michael met and conversed with a number of men while pointedly excluding me from their conversations. At one point right around half four, I thought a heard a faint noise in the distance, but no one in the pub reacted, and the silence continued. About forty-five minutes later, Holmes and Jimmy entered the pub.

"How did it go?" Michael asked.

"About as well as could be expected," Holmes replied.

"If you don't mind, Mr. Fergus, I'd like to hear what Jimmy has to say."

"It was quite the blast," he laughed, chuckling at his own witticism. "We was standing about a block away, when the bomb went off and half the windows on the ground floor blew out."

"You saw this with your own eyes?"

"I swear on me mother."

"How did you get the bomb into the house?"

"I hate to admit it, but I'll give credit where credit is due, he's a clever one" said Jimmy. "We were walking along Horse Guards Road, when Fergus spots this youngster. So he tells me to go lean on the lamppost.

"Then he says, 'Hey boy, would you like to like to earn two shillings?'

"The lad says 'Sure t'ing,' and Fergus tells him how he has two packages that must be delivered by half four, but he's got an important meeting in five minutes. He asks if the lad has a mate but the boy says no. With that he turns and pretends to notice me

54

standin' there. I was just a few feet away and so he says, 'You. How'd you like to make two bob?'

"We'd talked about it on the way over, and I knew what I was s'posed to do, so I got the package and the address and headed for Horse Guard Road. I watched as Fergus slid his envelope under the ribbon of the other box, and told the boy, 'Make certain that this gets to 10 Downing Street within ten minutes. Tell anyone who asks that it's a special delivery for the Prime Minister from Whitehall. Do you understand?'

"The boy says yes, grabs his shillings and heads for the Prime Minister's residence. After Fergus caught up to me, we put my package back in his satchel, crossed the street and watched from a distance as the boy rang the bell and handed the package to the butler. Not ten minutes later there's a tremendous explosion and all the windows blew out and smoke was billowing from the ground floor. We didn't stick around but came right back here."

"Well done, Mr. Fergus. You're a man of your word and I keep mine as well." With that he reached into his pocket and handed Holmes another fistful of notes. "There's the rest of your money."

Holmes counted it and thanked Michael. As we prepared to leave, Michael said, "I might 'ave another job for you. Let me see what the papers say about all this tomorrow. If everyt'ing went as planned and you are interested, meet me here tomorrow night at seven."

Holmes feigned indifference and said only, "Let me check my schedule and see if I'm free. If I'm here, we can talk. If I'm not, feel free to start without me."

Chapter 7

My mind was racing with questions, but I held my tongue until we had regained the safety of our flat. Once we had settled in front of the fire, I peppered Holmes with questions. "Holmes, what did the envelope say that Michael looked at? And weren't you lucky to find a boy to deliver your ticking bomb? And what happens now?"

"First things first, the envelope I showed Michael was a piece of official government stationary which I obtained from Mr. Orr. It said simply, 'The Rt Hon William Ewart Gladstone MP, The Prime Minister.' However, for a return address, I wrote 'The Rt Hon Hugh Childers, Chancellor of the Exchequer.' I was pretty certain Michael would be impressed, and I had already made arrangements for the package to be accepted.

"As for your second question. You know I that a carefully organized plan is far superior to luck. I had arranged for Wiggins to meet me there at exactly ten minutes after the hour. As soon as the package was received, it was submerged in a large tub of water they had waiting."

"Then what on Earth exploded?"

"That was a rather elaborate ruse crafted by Brocks Fireworks. They devised some simple detonating shells that sounded loud but damaged only the windows. Add in several large smoke bombs and the illusion is complete. The rest of the room was protected by a large curved sheet of steel to direct the blast outwards. As you might have guessed, the steel was invisible from Downing Street. Think of it as a bit of legerdemain designed to fool one person and one person only."

"Jimmy," I exclaimed.

"Exactly," replied Holmes. "Now with regard to your final question – What happens now? In truth, that remains to be seen. I am counting on the members of the press to be their usual lethargic selves and report everything they are told without really looking into anything. If they do a good job, and I am confident they will, we should see our standing in the Brotherhood improve considerably.

Holmes proved to be as good as his word, and the next morning as we walked to work at the docks, all the newsboys were screaming "Bomb blast at Downing Street," "Premier narrowly escapes assassination" and "Fenians continue reign of terror." In the afternoon as we returned home, it was more of the same. "I must say that is rather what I expected," remarked Holmes as we walked towards our flat.

When we turned the corner from Commercial Road onto Weyhill, the sisters, Jenny and Julie, were waiting for us. "Mr. Fergus," said Julie, "I have some news for you."

"You girls should be inside; it's quite chilly," I chided them.

"There is a young man in your flat. He got there about an hour ago and let himself in," exclaimed Jenny.

"I think he is waiting for you," added Julie.

Holmes thanked the girls and gave them each a shilling then he bid them go inside and get warm. "Obviously, something has come up," said Holmes. "We were supposed to meet at seven, and it's not even six yet."

"We could leave him there and just go straight to the Ten Bells," I suggested.

"I'm almost inclined to agree with you, but I must admit that I have a strong desire to find out exactly what they want."

I reluctantly followed Holmes. When we reached the flat, he entered first and from my position behind him, I couldn't see anything. Suddenly, I heard him laugh. "Wiggins, you rascal, what are you doing here?"

"I brought a message from Mrs. 'udson, who told me to tell you it was very important," so saying, he handed Holmes an envelope.

"How did you get in, lad?" I asked.

Looking at me with a sly smile, Wiggins replied, "Mr. 'Olmes ain't the only one what can pick a lock. I waited outside for nearly an hour in the cold and then I decided to just let myself in."

"Well done, my boy," replied Holmes. He then proceeded to read the letter over several times. Finally, he looked at Wiggins and said, "I don't want to put anything in writing. Tell Mrs. Hudson to inform the gentleman who sent this that he should take no action until he hears from me. Can you remember that?"

"No problem, guv," replied Wiggins.

Having got the fire started, Holmes carefully burned the note, stirring the ashes to make certain that no portion of it could be retrieved.

After Wiggins had departed, it struck me that the boy had known the location of this bolt-hole and I hadn't. I wondered if he knew where they all were.

As I turned to Holmes, he stated, "Wiggins knows the address of this and one other. He has known about them since before you and I met. I have not shared the locations of the others with anyone. However, if you'd like to know, I'd be happy to tell you."

"It's not important, Holmes, and I respect your privacy. Now, what was that letter all about?"

"Mr. Orr had written to say, one of the men they have working undercover has come up with what he believes is a clue to the identity of the new bomb-maker. He wanted to know if they should try to take him into custody when he arrives in this country from Ireland."

"And you told him not to?" I replied incredulously.

"For the moment. If he is arrested, there will just be someone else to take his place. I want to see what he knows and if he can lead us anywhere. The sooner we end this reign of terror, the better for everyone involved."

"Except for the Irish," I replied.

"I believe that eventually the Irish question will be resolved in their favor, but I'm afraid it may be years before that occurs. Right now, my concern is ending the bloodshed and the loss of life – on both sides."

"I think we had best make our way to the Ten Bells. We don't want to keep Michael waiting."

"Right you are, Watson."

As we entered the pub, there was a feeling of *bonhomie* among most of the men in the pub. As we made our way to the table, a few clapped Holmes on the back. One or two muttered, "Well done!"

Michael was all smiles. "It appears you are as good as your word, Mr. Fergus. Unfortunately, I'm given to understand that the

Prime Minister had left the room just a moment or two before the explosion. More's the pity."

"He is trying to help you," replied Holmes.

"But his help hasn't got us anywhere, now has it?"

"Better the devil you know ..." I added.

Seeing that this could continue indefinitely, Holmes quickly changed the subject, "You didn't ask to meet to congratulate me," said Holmes. "So how may I be of further assistance?"

"You are direct. I like that in a man, so, I'll be equally forthright. So far, our bombs have been ineffective. Yes, the people of London are scared, but the government has yet to take up the question of Home Rule for Ireland, despite the best efforts of Mr. Parnell in Parliament. You are familiar with the political machinations in play, I trust, Mr. Fergus."

"I understand that Gladstone is in favor of home rule."

"Yes, but then Mr. Gladstone could soon be gone and while the number of Irish patriots elected to Parliament is growing, they are still a distinct minority. No, I'm afraid we have to continue down this path, but maybe in a somewhat different direction perhaps, until the government recognizes the legitimacy of our cause."

"So where do I come in?" asked Holmes.

"I'm tinkin' it's time we changed our tactics. I want to continue the bombings but in a different way. I want them to be more intense, and far more effective and frequent. Yesterday, you showed them that even their Prime Minister is not beyond our reach. We need to drive that message home – no one is safe – day and night until the government is forced to give us our freedom."

"I can certainly appreciate your point," said Holmes, "but your tactics could have the opposite effect and force the government to dig in its heels. And, you never know what they might do to those still living in Ireland."

"I've considered that, Mr. Fergus, but in all honesty, there isn't much more misery they can inflict upon the people of Ireland. Truth be told, I can't see another way forward. Diplomacy hasn't worked. And Mr. Swift proved with his 'Modest Proposal' that you can't embarrass these people. Since we can't wage open warfare, we have to resort to guerilla tactics. Are you a student of history, Mr. Fergus?"

"I can't say that I am."

"Then I'll avoid boring you with the story of Quintus Fabius Maximus, except to say that we're going to employ his tactics, only in a more refined way."

"As I said, I'll do wat needs doin' – if the price is right."

"I will make it worth your while, Mr. Fergus, I assure you."

"And you'll take care of me mate as well?" Holmes asked, nodding towards me.

"Of course, but he can't expect the same rate of pay as yourself."

"As long as it beats a day's wages at the docks," I said. "I'm tired of hauling and lifting and breaking my back from mornin' 'til night for a few shillings."

"Oh, I think we can pay a bit more than the docks," said Michael. "Now, gentlemen, we are going to have a small gathering tomorrow night. I should like you both to attend. Think of it as a planning meeting." He then gave us an address on Turner

Street. "Be there at 11. The meeting will be in the cellar; the door is in the rear."

"We'll be on time," replied Holmes, as he rose and prepared to leave.

"Let me buy you and Hamish a pint before you go? You've earned it."

So we sat back down and when everyone had their ale, Michael said "To the green, white and gold! Slainte!" he took a long swallow and then added, "May this be the beginning of a long and prosperous partnership."

After we had finished, Michael offered us another round, but Holmes declined and we were soon on our way. As we exited the pub, a young boy sprinted past us on Commercial Road. When we reached the flat, Holmes knelt and checked the position of the cricket ball, then he held a finger to his lips indicating that I should be quiet. Upon entering he looked around but said nothing.

After we were seated in our chairs, I said, "Michael seemed quite pleased with you."

"Yes, but he's still suspicious."

"Why do you say that?"

"Watson, he only stood us those rounds so that he could have one of his confederates search the flat while we were in the Ten Bells. That's why he offered us a second round."

"How can you be so sure?"

"Do you recall the lad who sprinted by us when we left the pub?"

"Yes, what about him?"

"I am certain he was assigned to head back here when he saw us leave the pub and warn his cohort that we were on the way home. Besides, the ball has moved," he said pointing to the corner.

"What were they looking for?"

"Perhaps more dynamite, although I am inclined to think they were looking for anything that might compromise us. These men are playing a very high-stakes game, and they haven't lasted this long by being careless."

"So what are we to do?"

"We don't do anything differently; we just carry on and we'll see how much longer we have to play this game."

"Well, it can't end too soon for me, my friend."

"I agree, Watson, but I want to be the one who determines the conclusion that we reach."

"One more thing, Holmes. What did Michael mean when he toasted the green, white and gold?"

"He was referring to the new Irish flag that is a tricolor with the green representing the Irish Catholics, the orange is for the Protestants and the white is for peace."

"But if it's orange why say gold? That's what I found confusing."

"He was being poetic to a degree. They refer to the orange as gold – it's a sort of homage to an earlier flag that featured a golden harp against a green background – somewhat like the Brotherhood's own standard."

"The Brotherhood has its own colors?"

"Indeed, their flag features a golden sunburst on a green background. In their language it's called *An Gal Gréine*."

I went to sleep that night dreaming of flags and explosions and wondering what the future might bring.

The next day we worked at the docks and ate a quiet dinner in the Prospect of Whitby. I said little during the meal and Holmes even less.

As we walked home through a fine mist that added to the chill in the air, Holmes said, "We shall leave for the meeting around half ten. Until then, there is little to do. Why don't you rest before we go?"

"And what about you?"

"I have a bit of business to which I must attend. Also, I want to review everything in my mind. I cannot explain this nagging feeling that I have overlooked or missed something."

I knew all too well Holmes would never be satisfied until he had everything neatly arranged in his mind, so I didn't argue with him. After we had finished our meal, he left and I decided to take his advice and enjoy a short nap.

I awoke to find Holmes gently shaking me, "Time to go, old man. Splash some water on your face. We just have time for a cup of tea if you'd like one."

"I'm fine, Holmes, Just give me two minutes."

A few minutes later we were on our way to Turner Street. As we walked, I said, "Did you ever come up with the thing you thought you might have missed?"

"I'm afraid not. I tried reviewing the entire evening in detail, but to no avail. Still, I believe it will come to me eventually – sooner rather than later, I hope."

"By the way, I meant to ask you, who was that Roman Michael mentioned."

"Quintus Fabius Maximus?"

"I believe that was the name."

"He was a Roman general during the second Punic War. Realizing that Hannibal was a skilled commander and aware that the Romans could not win a pitched battle, he fought a war of attrition against Hannibal, harassing his soldiers and attacking his supply lines. Although his strategy was derided at the time, it could be said that Rome survived only because of his unorthodox tactics."

"Sounds rather like what the Irish are attempting to do to us."

Holmes stopped right in the middle of the street. Fortunately, as it was late, there was no traffic. He stood there lost in thought for fully three minutes. Finally, I began to see just the beginnings of a smile crease his face.

"Thank you, Watson. You have provided the solution for that nettlesome problem that was gnawing at me."

Not quite certain exactly what I had done, I accepted the rare compliment from Holmes and said only, "Thank you."

"You have no idea what you have done, do you?"

"Truthfully, no."

Holmes then explained how I was invaluable as a sounding board. "You always see the surface, my friend, and you often remind me to look beneath it – something I am always encouraging you to do."

"I still don't understand."

"You are an educated man, a military man and yet you are unfamiliar with the heroics of Quintus Fabius Maximus. So how is it that Michael seems well aware of the Roman general's accomplishments? Moreover, as you so rightly pointed out, Michael is emulating his tactics as he wages his own war against the British government – and by extension, its people."

By now we were turning into Turner Street. Holmes looked at me in the near darkness and said, "I'm starting to wonder if perhaps two can play at that game. Here we are number 32." Holmes then turned to me and in a low whisper said, "No more of this for now, but thank you again, old friend."

So saying, he turned and walked down the alley, heading for the rear of the house where Michael had told us we would find the door to the cellar.

Chapter 8

Holmes knocked on the door, and a voice from inside barked, "Who's there?"

"It's Fergus and Hamish," replied Holmes.

Soon Jimmy, holding a dark lantern, cautiously opened the door. After he had shone his light upon us, he said, "You alone?"

"Of course we are," replied Holmes.

"It's about time. We been waitin' on you two."

I considered pointing out that we were actually a few minutes early but decided against it.

We then descended a few steps and found Michael and three other men, in addition to Jimmy, sitting at a long table. The room was damp and cold and the only illumination was provided by two sputtering candles, sitting a few feet apart in the middle of the table. We sat across from the men flanking Michael; as a result, neither us was directly in front of Michael.

"So glad you could join us," Michael said.

"What's all this about?" Holmes demanded. "I've a long day on the docks tomorrow, and I need me rest."

"Perhaps you'll not be goin' back to the docks," Michael replied. "Perhaps you'll be comin' to work for me."

"Only if you can make it worth my while," countered Holmes.

Turning to the other men at the table, Michael said, "You see – a true mercenary at heart. That's what we need – more professionals."

"Can we afford 'im?" asked one of the men with a thick brogue.

"Who might you be?" asked Holmes.

"No names, please," said Michael.

"That hardly seems fair. After all, he knows my name, I'm sure."

"Yes, he does, but you don't need to know his – at least not yet."

"It still doesn't seem quite fair," said Holmes sulkily.

"Enough," said Michael. "You're here because we want to make use of your skills – for which we are more than willing to pay. If you were one of us, you'd be doin' your part for the love of Eire, but you're not. I don't like it, but I accept it.

"Now, shall we get down to business?" When no one spoke, Michael continued, "I mean to step up the bombing campaign. If possible, I want to have at least one bomb to explode every day for a month, perhaps two months. If you're willing, Mr. Fergus, you'll be responsible for constructing 15 bombs, choosing the targets and arranging the detonations."

"You said every day fer a month. Last time I checked there was at least thirty days in most months."

"You are not our only bomb-maker, Mr. Fergus, but you have proven your skill. Now do you want to accept my offer?"

"That depends? What's the pay?"

"We will pay you £50 for each bomb that we deem successful."

"I like the number, but we've probably got very different definitions of success."

"If it causes a disruption, if it terrifies the public, then I'd call it successful."

"Well that seems generous enough. When do you want to start?"

"I have a very definite date in mind, but I am waiting for money from America and supplies from home. As soon as they arrive, hopefully within a fortnight, we can meet again and discuss the particulars."

"So we're workin' on the docks 'til we hear from you?" I asked.

It was almost as though they had forgot that I was in the room. Suddenly, they all looked at me, Michael smiled and said, "That sums it up quite nicely. Goodnight gentlemen, I'll be in touch."

We left the basement and walked back to our room in silence.

After we had got settled and lit our pipes, I said to Holmes, "That was a rather tense affair. He could have asked us that in the pub. Why such a clandestine meeting?"

"I believe the two on either side of Michael are his masters in some way or at the very least, his equals. The meeting offered them an opportunity to see us, perhaps to make certain that we aren't police masquerading as Fenians."

"It all seems unnecessary to me."

"You realize, of course, that if I hadn't accepted their offer, we wouldn't be sitting here now."

"What do you mean?"

"Each of the two men flanking Michael was holding a shotgun under the table – one aimed at you and the other at me. We were either going to accept their offer, or we were going to meet our maker."

"My word, Holmes. How do you know that?"

"You will recall that our two chairs were positioned directly opposite theirs. You might also have noticed that Jimmy and the other fellow never stood behind us, rather they were off to one side at either end of the table. At one point, when they turned their attention to you, I was able to fish my silver cigarette case from my pocket and using it as mirror, I managed a glimpse under the table."

"Holmes, I think we should tell everything we know to the Special Irish Branch at Scotland Yard. They can keep these men under surveillance and stop them before they attempt anything."

"Just as they stopped all those other bombings? No, Watson, it simply won't do. Besides, there is or will soon be a second bomb-maker on the scene, and we can provide no information about that person. I'm afraid we must play this hand out."

"But Holmes, you don't even know where these men live!"

"Which again speaks to your point. What would we tell the Yard? That we know that this man who calls himself Michael who we met in the Ten Bells is planning to detonate more bombs? We have no proof. Besides, I'll know where they reside soon enough."

"How will you learn that?"

"While you were napping, I met with Wiggins and arranged for the Irregulars to follow everyone who was at that meeting. He will report to me tomorrow evening. Fortunately, we have time before Michael intends to put his plan into action. Hopefully, we will be able to learn about this new bomb-maker and his plans so that we can take steps to bring their operation to a standstill.

"Now, let's enjoy our pipes. We have a long day ahead of us tomorrow and quite possibly a longer night."

"I can't wait to get back to Baker Street."

"I share that sentiment, old friend, but with so much hanging in the balance our petty desires seem trivial, almost selfish, do they not?"

I couldn't argue with any of his sentiments, so I merely replied, "Do you never tire of being right?"

Holmes merely smiled and said nothing. Although we finished our pipes in an amiable silence, I must admit that my mind was racing the entire time as I tried to imagine all the difficulties and impediments on the road to our goal.

The following evening about seven, there was a knock on the door. I went to it and asked, "Who's there?"

"It's me, Doctor Watson," I heard Wiggins whisper. "I need to see Mister 'Olmes."

I opened the door and let the boy in.

"I assume you have news for me," said Holmes.

"'Deed, I do," replied Wiggins. "After you and Dr. Watson passed, I waited about a 'alf 'our then this Michael fellow you described comes out. He says good night to his mates, and then I followed him down Commercial to an 'ouse on Folgate Street, Number 28. He let himself in with a key, and I waited nearly an hour – it was bloody cold, too – but 'e never came back out."

"Did you wait for the lights to come on?" Holmes asked.

"He's on the first floor, in the front on the right side."

"What of the other two men?"

"Evans and Skilt followed two of 'em to a 'ouse on Varden Street. I think they must share a room 'cause they went in together and no one came back out. They saw the lights come on and go out about a half hour later. The room is on the ground floor in the back."

"And the others?"

"Dicky and Francis tailed them to a roomin' 'ouse on Newark Street, No. 14. They share a room too, I think – first floor, back right if you're looking at it from the front."

"Well done, my lad! Well done!" said Holmes as he handed the boy some coins. "I need the man you followed watched day and night. Work in pairs, and if he meets someone, split up, with one of you following Michael and the other the person he meets. Take notes of where he goes and get descriptions of the people he meets. There's double the usual wages, so I'm counting on you and the rest of the lads."

"We won't let ya down, Mr. 'Olmes. You have my word."

"You can bring your reports here – just remember to use the rear entrance from now on. Or if there is nothing crucial, you can leave them with Mrs. Hudson. I'll be checking with her every other day."

"Righto, guv," said Wiggins. "You'll hear from me or one of the other lads tomorrow."

"And Wiggins, two more things: First, tell the boys to dress warmly. They are going to have some long, cold days and nights in front of them."

"Yes, guv, and what else?"

"From now on, and this is very important, no more names when you knock at the door. If the wrong person were to overhear…" and Holmes let the words hang there.

"Sorry, Mr. 'Olmes. I'll do better from now on. Only thing is some of the lads don't have warm coats or gloves."

Holmes then handed Wiggins a few notes and said, "If someone needs a hat or a coat or a pair of gloves, buy it for him. This job is too important to let a piece of clothing prove its undoing. You know what they say Wiggins, 'For want of a nail, the shoe was lost…'"

Wiggins looked at Holmes quizzically then said only, "W'atever you say, Mr. 'Olmes." With that, he put his hat on and was out the door.

"I think your Shakespeare was lost on the lad."

"Perhaps, but it will give him something to think about, and if I know Wiggins he will figure it out."

"That may be, but now that you know where Michael lives, what's our next move?"

"I think we need to employ the tactics of one Quintus Fabius Maximus."

"What on Earth do you mean?"

"I mean to harass him, to attack his supply lines. I mean to locate the source of his funding. And most important, I need to discover the identity of the other bomb-maker."

"Pray tell, how do you plan to accomplish all those tasks?"

"I am formulating a plan, Watson. Right now, it is in its infancy, but much of it depends upon the information that Wiggins provides."

"What do you hope to learn from Wiggins?"

"I need to know where Michael banks, what telegraph office he uses, what other people he sees. Young Wiggins and the lads will earn their wages over the next several days, of that you can rest assured."

The next two days passed slowly. Each evening Wiggins or one of the other Irregulars would report to Holmes. By the third day, we had learned that Michael frequented the telegraph office at St. Katharine Docks, banked at Barclays, and was a regular at just about all the pubs in Whitechapel. We also learned that he had no discernable source of income.

Holmes was collecting his precious data, but on the afternoon of the third day, everything changed. We were returning home from the docks, and I was looking forward to a quiet evening with a book.

As we entered our building, Holmes held up a hand to stop me. He turned with a finger to his lips. Cupping his hands over my ear, he whispered, "Someone is in our flat. The door is ajar.

"I'm going to go out and come in through the back. When you see me at the end of the hall, rattle the doorknob and slam the door as though you had just arrived home."

A few minutes later, I saw Holmes at the end of the hall, hiding in the shadows. Opening the door, I slammed it and said, "If I never lift another case of tea…"

All of sudden, Wiggins burst out of the flat, "Is that you. Doctor? Where is Mister …"

Holmes sprang forward and put his hand over the stunned boy's mouth. "No names, remember?" he said through his teeth.

Wiggins nodded that he understood, and the three of us made our way into the flat.

"You keep picking locks, and you just might get shot," I cautioned the boy.

"Why are you here, Wiggins?"

"I've got some important news," he exclaimed.

"Out with it," ordered Holmes.

"About an hour ago, I was following yer man, and Grogan was 'elpin'. He's been busy all day, meeting people, sending telegraphs, shopping…"

"The news, boy. Get to the news."

"So 'e goes into Victoria Park and he walks to the East Fishin' Lake where 'e takes a seat on a bench. He's sittin' there doin' nothin' when all of a sudden there's a 'uge explosion by the drinkin' fountain."

"The Burdett Coutts Fountain?" I asked incredulously.

"I don't know the right name of it; I just calls it the drinkin' fountain."

"The one with the four clock faces?" Holmes asked.

"That's the one. Only those clocks won't be workin' for a while."

"Was anyone hurt?" I asked.

"Can't say. After the blast, yer man just kinda smiled and headed for the nearest gate. He 'ailed a cab, and I 'eard him tell the driver the Ten Bells. I told Grogan to folla him, and I came right 'ere. I figured you'd wanna know."

"You have done well, Wiggins. Now, I need you to keep following that man, and it is more imperative than ever you not be seen."

"I'm never seen when I don't wants to be," the boy replied.

"Excellent! I'll wait for your next report tomorrow then." Holmes handed the boy some coins. As the youngster turned the doorknob, Holmes added, "And Wiggins, do be careful."

"You can count on me, Mister 'Olmes," he whispered.

When we were alone, I looked at Holmes and said, "What does this mean?"

"I'm not certain. There are several possibilities. Michael may have moved up the time-line for the bombings. He may have decided to delegate all the work to the other bomb-maker, or, and this is the one I am most hopeful for, the bombing was a test, just as my bomb at 10 Downing Street was a trial."

"Yes, but yours was controlled. Lord knows how many people were killed or injured with this one. And why Victoria Park?"

"Since it opened back in 1845, the park has been a gathering place for youngsters as it afforded them an unspoiled swath of green – so different from much of the rest of London. In the past few decades people of all political persuasions have been congregating there, much as they do at the Speakers' Corner in Hyde Park. Taken together and considering the amenities, many Londoners have begun referring to it as 'the people's park.'"

"So why bomb the fountain?"

"Most people in our fair city have no strong opinion one way or another about the Irish question. If you can rouse the ire of those people and convince them that the government's stance on Ireland is the cause of the bombings and the misery they are suffering is because of the bombings, you may be able to rally the masses to exert pressure on their MPs to side with the Irish."

"Holmes, that sounds almost like blackmail!"

"In a way it is, Watson. Our job is to end the extortion before it begins to find a foothold among the people."

"Perhaps we should go and see Michael right now. We know where he is."

"Unfortunately, old friend, the earliest we can do anything is tomorrow. By that time all of London will be talking about the attack as I am certain the papers will cover it."

"And what do we do tonight?"

"We make plans, and as we do we must allow for unforeseen contingencies. As far as I know, we – and the informants in the Irish Republican Brotherhood – are all that stand between these terrorists and a city slipping into chaos and possibly anarchy."

"Surely, you overstate the case?"

"Do I? The more bombs that are detonated, the more people are injured and killed, the more people are huddling in their homes in fear, the more likely Michael's campaign is likely to succeed. No, Watson, it falls on us to bring Michael and his cohorts to justice – by any means necessary."

Although I understood Holmes' words, it would be some time before I realized their full import.

Chapter 9

The following day I went to work at the docks, while Holmes, disguised once again as a nonconformist clergyman, visited the park to inspect the scene of the bombing. I didn't see him until that evening when we made our way to the Ten Bells. When we arrived, we found Michael holding court at his usual table in the rear. He waved us over and we joined him, Jimmy and two other fellows at their table.

"We need to talk," Holmes said.

"Anything you need to tell me, you can say in front of these men. I would trust them with my life."

Lowering his voice, Holmes leaned forward and said, "I suppose that was your bit of work in Victoria Park yesterday."

"I might know something about it," Michael replied with a sly grin.

"It would appear the supplies you were waiting on have arrived. Has the money?"

"Not yet. It's coming from America."

"You also said you were going to wait at least a fortnight, and two days later you blow up a fountain."

"I blew up nothing, Mr. Fergus. And we are going to wait until the date I have determined to begin the next stage of our campaign."

"Then what was yesterday all about?"

"Think of it as another test. Just as we had you prove yourself, I had to make certain Daire was up to snuff so to speak."

"Well, the fountain's still standin', so I'm not sure what to think. I'd like to meet this Daire and see what he had in mind."

"Don't you worry about meetin' Daire or anything else but the jobs I give you. I'll handle the rest."

"Will you be choosin' where the bombs go off or will I?"

"Does it make a difference?"

"It makes a big difference to me," replied Holmes. "You've seen how I work. I scout my targets and I plan accordingly. I don't just drop a bag and run like your boys have in the past."

"What are ya sayin' there?" interrupted Jimmy.

"I'm just sayin' that I wouldn't be here if you fellas knew anything about bombs and explosives. The boys who tried to blow up the bridge come to mind. Lots of noise, but no damage 'cept to some windows – and themselves." At that Holmes laughed and took a big swallow of ale.

I could see that Jimmy was seething, but Michael laid a hand on his arm to restrain him. "Those were our friends and comrades-in-arms, and you'd do better to speak of them with respect," cautioned Michael.

"No disrespect intended," replied Holmes. "I'm certain they were patriots and good soldiers, but they obviously lacked any degree of skill with regard to planting a bomb."

Michael looked at Jimmy and said, "You can't argue with that, I'm afraid."

"To patriots and soldiers," Jimmy exclaimed, hoisting his mug high.

"And to those who refuse to see the light, that they may in time see their way clear," Michael added.

It seemed an odd addition to me, but then I was not thoroughly versed in the fine art of Irish toasting.

After we had all drunk, Michael looked at Holmes and said, "Suppose you develop a list of fifteen targets and give the list to me to look over? Will that be satisfactory?"

"That'd be just grand," replied Holmes. "How many places do you really want on the list?"

Michael thought it over and then he said, "Well, since we might disagree on any number of them, give me a list of thirty. That way even if we can't agree on half you can still proceed. Can you do it in a week?"

"Only if Hamish and I quit the docks. Scouting all those locations will take time. Some of the ones I'm considerin' are only open durin' the day, and we still have rent to pay and other expenses."

"It's always about the money with you, isn't it Fergus?" asked Jimmy.

"You're hirin' me to do somethin' – somethin' that requires a degree of expertise. Unfortunately for you, such expertise comes at a price."

"How much more?" asked Michael.

"Well like I said, I've no love for the English, so jus' pay us what we'd earn at the docks? That fair?"

"I suppose so." With that Michael pulled a handful of notes from his pocket, counted off a few and handed them to Holmes. "Is there anything else, Mr. Fergus?"

"You'll provide the dynamite and the timers?"

Michael nodded, and Holmes continued, "Just make certain you buy better ones than you used last year."

I saw Michael redden, but Holmes continued undeterred, "Last February, you left bombs in luggage bags with timers in a number of railway cloak rooms. Among your targets were Victoria, Ludgate Hill, Charing Cross and Paddington. If I remember right, the only bomb to detonate was the one at Victoria. Admittedly, you did some damage there, but the other three bombs failed either because of faulty timers or the police discovered them in time. 'Tis hard to imagine how much more effective your campaign might be had they all gone off."

"You seem quite knowledgeable about our affairs," Michael said.

"When there's dynamite involved, I make it my business to know what's going on," Holmes countered.

"So what would you suggest?"

"I'll get the dynamite and the timers, and," here he looked at Jimmy and smiled, "there'll be no profit on my part."

"Why would you do that, when you appear to be all about the money?"

"Because I'm putting my life on the line here, and I prefer to work with equipment I can trust. I don't want to end up like so many of these anarchists who build bombs and end up blowing themselves up. And I certainly don't want to spend the rest of me life missin' parts of me hands." Gesturing towards the front, where the man who was missing parts of two fingers was sitting with another fellow, Holmes held up both his hands and said,

"Unlike that fella, I still have all my fingers and I'd like to keep 'em."

After everyone at the table had finished laughing, Michael said, "How much more?"

"I'll buy what I need for my 15 bombs and save the receipts. Will that work?"

"Seems fair enough," replied Michael with a degree of resignation in his voice.

"Suppose I need to get in touch with you in a hurry?" Holmes asked. "Where can I reach you?"

"If you need me, leave word here. Someone will know my whereabouts."

With that, they shook hands, Holmes and I finished our pints and we headed out into the night. "Well, that couldn't have gone better if I'd scripted it myself," he said after we had reached our flat and taken seats in front of the fireplace.

"How so?" I asked. "Aside from learning the first name of the other bomb-maker – Daire – what else have you determined?"

"Watson, I am disappointed. You know my methods, consider the flow of the conversation and its myriad implications."

"I must admit to being quite at sea, Holmes."

"You'll recall that I called into question the skill of the other bomb-maker. That set Michael to thinking."

"I'm still not following you."

"Initially, Michael asked me to develop a list of fifteen targets, which he once again repeated tonight. Then all of a sudden for no apparent reason he doubled the number to thirty on the pretext that we might disagree. While we may have opposite opinions about two or three targets, the chances are slim that we would disagree on half of them."

"He wants the rest for the other bomber," I exclaimed.

"Bravo!"

"What else have I overlooked?"

"Quite a bit I'm afraid. In your stories, you often illustrate my abilities by having me deduce all types of things from people's appearance or the mud stains on their trousers. Plotting conversations is a similar skill. I rehearse my remarks in my head and then try to anticipate the various responses they might engender."

"So what else did you plan tonight?"

"I questioned the timers the group has been using, which were quite often defective. He knows that the timer I used on my 'bomb' worked perfectly. After all, it detonated at the designated hour, and Jimmy and I are still alive."

"So that's why you offered to supply the timers."

"Exactly. If it becomes necessary I will provide Michael with the receipts for the equipment I purchase for my timers. However, I will not provide instructions. But more important, I am confident he will purchase the same items from the same shop. So while I can guarantee that the items he buys will look similar, I will find a way to render the timers he or Daire constructs inoperable if it comes to that."

"Still, you are taking a risk. If this other bomb-maker has any talent, he may be able to ascertain the changes you have made."

"Point taken, Watson. I shall have to give the notion some additional thought. As you know I constantly refine my plans, and there's no reason to stop now."

After a nightcap, we turned in, and in the morning, Holmes said, "I think we have been away from Baker Street long enough. Besides, there are people I need to see, and I can't very well keep meeting them dressed as a dockworker."

"What would you have me do?"

"I'll leave first dressed as I am. After I've gone out the front, wait five minutes and then leave via the back. If anyone is watching us, they will hopefully follow me. However, it is imperative you make certain you are not followed. When you arrive at Baker Street, enter through the tradesmen's entrance. Tell Mrs. Hudson I'll be along presently and ask her if dinner would be too much trouble."

"And what will you be doing?"

"This morning I plan to tour the Crystal Palace to see where we might place a bomb. Then I'll stop in at another of my refuges, change my attire into something a bit more presentable and pay a visit to the British Library."

"Another site for your list of targets, I presume."

"While it will certainly appear on my list, I have other business to which I must attend there."

"Holmes, be careful, lest something go wrong and these terrorists decide to make use of your list."

"You have my word, Watson. I shall take no undue chances."

Satisfied, I stood in the hall as Holmes went out the front; I waited approximately five minutes and then left through the rear door. I walked through the alley to Coke Street. From that point on, it was a most circuitous route that I took home, hiring and changing cabs on two different occasions, and finally entering Harrods, where I made certain, I wasn't being followed. As a result, I arrived at the tradesmen's entrance in the rear of 221 at almost two in the afternoon.

When I knocked at the door, Mrs. Hudson opened it, looked at me in my labourer's garb and said only, "Back from America already? And looking like that? Shall I bring some tea up, Doctor?"

I said nothing about her light sarcasm, but merely expressed my appreciation and inquired about dinner. "That won't be a problem, Doctor. Truth be told, with everything that's going on in the city, I must confess that I am glad you two are back."

I went upstairs where I washed, trimmed my beard and put on a clean shirt and collar. I had just finished when Mrs. Hudson arrived with the tea and a plate of warm scones as well as pots of strawberry jam and clotted cream. After several weeks of public house fare, I savored the light scones as well as the jam and cream.

When Mrs. Hudson arrived to clear away the plates, I looked at her and before I could speak, she said, "Don't worry, Doctor. This will be our little secret."

I smiled and thanked her. I spent the rest of the afternoon catching up on my correspondence and jotting down notes from our current investigation.

Shortly before six, I heard the front door open and a few minutes later I thought I recognized Holmes' tread as he ascended the stairs. A moment later, he threw open the door and entered, stopping by the rack to hang up his coat and hat. He seemed in a jovial mood, and my suspicions were confirmed when he said, "I hope your afternoon was as profitable as mine, Doctor."

"I caught up with the post, and you will find all your letters at your place at the dinner table. Then I set about jotting down more notes for our current case."

As he sat down to the dinner table where I had been sitting earlier, he picked up his mail and said, "You did ask Mrs. Hudson about dinner?"

"I did. She plans to serve at seven."

"Will you have any room after the scones and jam?"

"What on Earth? How could you possibly know?"

"As soon as I entered the house, I could smell the aroma of freshly baked goods. You know you are not the only fan of her scones. However, when I stopped in the kitchen to inquire about the results of her culinary efforts, she informed me that they were all gone. Since she always bakes at least a dozen, I can only assume that what she, the maid and Billy didn't eat somehow found their way up here."

"So you guessed!"

"Watson, I never guess. You know me better than that. I deduced."

"And pray tell, upon what data did you base your deduction?"

"You left your napkin on your chair. Unless I am gravely mistaken, there are a few small red splotches upon it. Since you haven't shaved but only trimmed your beard, I think I can safely assume those are traces of strawberry jam."

"Well done, Holmes."

"Besides, he continued, there are a few small crumbs on the table that either you or Mrs. Hudson missed."

I could only sit there red-faced – figuratively, I hoped – and marvel at my friend's abilities to discern the truth from the slightest of clues. We settled into an amiable silence as Holmes perused his correspondence. After about fifteen minutes, he rose and threw most of it on the fire.

"I should tell you that I am expecting guests after supper," he advised me.

"Oh?"

"Yes, I've asked Lestrade to stop by, and he may be bringing one of the officers from the Special Irish Branch."

Formed in 1883 in the midst of the bombing campaign, the Special Irish Branch had been established in an attempt to bring the Fenian bombers to justice. All of the officers recruited had Irish backgrounds, and their success was difficult to gauge because they were so secretive about their activities. I knew a number of men had been assigned to the docks, presumably in an effort to detect any explosives being smuggled in. I know Holmes thought the move short-sighted as he pointed out that travelers from Ireland could land at any number of ports – Liverpool, Portsmouth, Southampton and New Haven, to name a few – and then smuggle their dynamite into London via rail, but then no one had asked his opinion on this matter.

We had just finished a delicious dinner of chicken and dumplings and were enjoying an after-dinner brandy when I heard the bell. Footsteps on the stairs were soon followed by a knock on the door. "Come in, Lestrade," Holmes bellowed.

I turned to see Inspector Lestrade enter, followed by another man. Lestrade shook our hands and then introduced his companion as Inspector Robert Smith, one of the men who had been selected for service in the Special Irish Branch.

"Finally, back from America. I won't say I've missed you, Mr. Holmes, but there's them that has. And truth be told, I would have liked to compare notes with you in one or two instances."

After Lestrade had finished. Smith stepped forward, extended his hand and said, with just a hint of a brogue, "It's a pleasure to meet you, Mr. Holmes." Turning to me and shaking my hand, he added, "And you as well, Dr. Watson."

"What can we do for you, Holmes?" asked Lestrade.

"Without going into too much detail, I have been asked by Her Majesty's government to look into the Fenian bombings with an eye toward ending their reign of terror.

"To date, Watson and I have made some small degree of progress, and I was wondering if you might able to supply any additional information, Inspector Smith."

"What makes you think that, Holmes?" asked Lestrade.

"I was given to understand that you have been able to infiltrate the group here in London," replied Holmes casually.

"Groups," countered Smith. "There are more than one; in fact, we know of at least three."

"Are they all involved in the bombings?" asked Holmes.

"To varying degrees. There is one group that appears to be taking the lead while the others are ready and willing to supply men and a bit of money, should it become necessary," said Smith.

"In which groups have you been able to place informants?" I asked.

"We have men in two of the groups, but we have not been able to infiltrate that lead faction I mentioned. The problem is that none of my men has been able to secure any type of leadership position, and all of the leaders are quite close-mouthed. To say they play things close to the vest would be an understatement."

"Which of the groups you alluded to is the driving force behind the bombings?"

"It's a group based in Whitechapel, and its leader is a man named Michael Byrne." I noticed Smith had used the Irish pronunciation for Michael, which sounded like "Mee-Hawl."

"He's a right, smart fella," Smith continued. "A former soldier, he served with the Royal Irish Regiment and saw action in the Second Anglo-Afghan War. Unfortunately, despite his heroics on the battlefield, he struck a superior officer. As a result, he was court-martialed and dishonorably discharged."

"Would I be wrong in assuming the officer was English?" I inquired.

"Not at all, Doctor."

"What do we know about his family?" asked Holmes.

"His father was a tenant farmer, who was evicted by an absentee landlord – an English aristocrat," added Smith. "If I had to guess I'd say Trevelyan was involved in the eviction."

"I'm familiar with the actions of Trevelyan," said Holmes.

"So it's safe to say there's no love lost between Byrne and the English?" asked Holmes.

"That seems a fair statement," replied Smith.

"What have you learned about the group's plans?" asked Holmes.

"Not much. As I said, that's the one group we haven't been able to insert anyone in, so all of our intelligence about it is second-hand and thus somewhat suspect. Still, we know they have a new bomb-maker, fella by the name of Fergus. We believe he is the man responsible for the bomb at 10 Downing Street. He may also be responsible for the blast at the fountain in Victoria Park the other day."

Obviously even the Special Irish Branch had been kept in the dark about Downing Street. I could only assume the Prime Minister's office had decided it were best if our actions remained secret. (A few years later I learned that with Mycroft's urging, Downing Street had agreed to play along with that bit of deception.)

"What do you know about this Fergus fellow?" asked Holmes.

"Not a great deal, I'm afraid. We believe he works on the docks and lives somewhere in Whitechapel or Spitalfields."

"That's all you have?"

"You have to understand, Mr. Holmes. Our resources are quite limited. Right now I have three men trying to do the work of ten. They can't follow everyone all the time. Just give me a few more weeks and we'll know everything we need to know about him – including his shoe size and how he takes his tea."

"Anything else about this group of which I should be aware?" asked Holmes.

"We believe they are waiting for another bomb-maker to arrive. Obviously, it always pays to have a spare."

"True," Holmes offered, "or they might be planning to step things up. After all, their political agenda appears to be at a dead end, so this may turn out to be their only recourse."

"That's certainly a possibility," agreed Smith.

"If you could keep us informed about the group and its leaders, I would be most appreciative."

"Should something develop, you'll be the first to know – right after the officials at the Yard."

"Thank you, Inspector Smith. And thank you, Lestrade," Holmes said.

I showed the men to the door, and after I'd heard the front door close, I turned to Holmes and said, "Why didn't you tell Smith that you and Fergus are one."

"The fewer people who know our business, the better," he replied. "Suppose he passed that information along to one of his informants, I have to think that man would look at us differently and treat us differently. All it would take would be one slight misstep and that might well be the end of Fergus and Hamish. As you have noted, Doctor, Michael and his cohorts are not men to be trifled with."

The next several days were quite relaxing for me as I had little to do. Holmes preferred to conduct his reconnaissance alone; as a result, I was able to attend to a great many personal matters which I had neglected while we were living in Whitechapel.

One afternoon, Holmes came home in a rather jaunty mood, which I found odd since he was wearing his clergyman's disguise. "You seem rather chipper this afternoon," I hazarded.

"My work is done for the moment," replied Holmes.

"You mean you've finished your list?"

"Indeed, I have," he replied, handing me a sheet of paper.

As I perused it, I was stunned by the breadth of the targets Holmes had selected. Among the places he had compiled were the floor of the London Stock Exchange, the Reading Room at the British Library, Poets' Corner in Westminster Abbey and the gallery at St. Paul's Cathedral. When I finished, I said, "Are you sure you don't want to include Buckingham Palace?"

"I had considered it," he remarked, "but then I decided against it."

I couldn't tell whether he was serious, so I simply said, "If you were truly in their employ, there wouldn't be much of London left standing when you had finished your work."

"I'm going to take that as a compliment. Now, take a look at this other list."

He then handed me a second sheet which I perused. "These are quite different." Among the possibilities he had included were the Crystal Palace, Nelson's Column at Trafalgar Square, Paddington Station and the HMS Devastation.

"Yes, and therein lies the key. The first sheet contains all the places they should be bombing if their goal is to frighten the citizens of London. The second merely offers the same type of targets they have already attempted."

"I see that, but what is the point of compiling two such different lists?"

"I will present the list of my intended targets first, so that I can gauge Michael's reaction. However, I will make certain that one way or another both lists fall into his hands."

"Why on Earth would you do such a thing?"

"Surely, Watson, even you can see where this is heading."

"I'm afraid I am at a loss."

"Well do give it some thought. I believe it's a rather straightforward affair although I must admit there are a few twists and turns."

"Holmes, must you always be so mysterious? I am doing my best to keep up, but you certainly aren't making it any easier."

"I'll give you a suggestion. Consider the differences between the Poets' Corner and Trafalgar Square and then weigh the differences between the Reading Room and the HMS Devastation."

As you might have guessed, Holmes' hint proved to be no help at all.

Chapter 10

I was preparing myself to return to the daily deprivations of our Whitechapel existence, when two days later Holmes reminded me, "Don't forget, we have a very important meeting with Michael tomorrow night."

"Has it been a week already?"

"Actually, it has been eight days. So enjoy a hearty dinner – it may be your last for a while – forget to shave and I shall wake you at five."

"What are we going to be doing at such an ungodly hour?"

"We need to resume our old lives at the docks, I'm afraid."

Having resigned myself to my fate, I savoured every morsel of the meal Mrs. Hudson had prepared – a perfectly cooked joint of roast beef with roasted potatoes and runner beans. We were enjoying a brandy when I heard the bell ring. A minute later, I could discern footfalls on the stairs.

"I wonder what could bring Lestrade here at this hour," remarked Holmes.

That was followed by a soft rapping on the door, to which Holmes replied, "Come in, Lestrade."

"I'm glad I could catch you at home, Mr. Holmes."

"What can I do for you, Inspector?"

"First, let me give you a piece of information. According to Smith's informant, the new bomb-maker has finally arrived. Unfortunately, no one has met nor even seen him so a description is impossible."

"I can't say I'm surprised, Inspector; after all, we have been expecting him. If anything, I'm wondering what took him so long to get here."

"Unfortunately, that's all Smith's men have been able to learn. Oh, there is one more thing – Smith's man believes the new bomber is living somewhere in or near the Whitechapel district."

"That was to be expected. Now, what can I do for you, Inspector? You could have sent a telegram or written a note to the same effect, but the fact that you decided to deliver the news yourself leads me to believe that you are here in some other capacity than as a mere messenger."

"Still up to your old tricks, Holmes. Well, you've caught me out fair and square."

I had to chuckle at Lestrade's discomfort. "I should have thought you would know better, Inspector."

Ignoring my comment, Lestrade turned to Holmes and said, "It's a nasty bit of business, Mr. Holmes. Over the past few weeks, there have been a series of robberies in some of the high-end shops along Oxford Street. They've also targeted merchants in Piccadilly and on St. James Street. It appears that a new gang is operating in that area. We originally thought the thieves might be members of Forty Elephants, but at least two of the shop owners swear they were robbed by men."

"I wish I could help you, Lestrade, but I find myself rather busy at the moment as you might imagine."

"I can understand that, Mr. Holmes. But you will keep your ear to the ground?"

"Of course," replied Holmes. "You have no clues?"

"Only this," replied Lestrade, pulling a small item from his pocket. He handed it to Holmes, who pulled out his lens and began to examine it carefully. I watched as Holmes turned the small stone over in his hand and then scrutinised the reverse.

"Any thoughts, Mr. Holmes?"

"It's marble, Inspector, and it has been smoothed and polished. Obviously, it's a talisman of some kind. How did you come by it?"

"A clerk in Fortnum and Mason was chasing one of the shoplifters. During the struggle to recover a silver teapot, he managed to grab the thief's coat and rip the pocket. Along with a few coins and a set of rosary beads, this fell out."

"So the thief got away with the teapot and you were left with rosary beads and a stone," I added. "Hardly seems like a fair trade."

"Left or right, Lestrade?"

"Pardon, Holmes?"

"Did the clerk rip the pocket from the left side of the thief's coat or the right?"

"Does it really make a difference?" asked Lestrade.

"It might, Inspector. How often have I tried to stress to you the importance of details? At any rate, if you could find out, I would appreciate it."

"I'll ask the clerk myself," Lestrade promised.

"And then just send a note here."

"Will do."

"One more thing, Lestrade, may I hold onto this? I have some people I'd like to have examine it. They may be able to shed some light on it."

"It is evidence, but it's not doing me any good, so what's the harm? By the by, how was your trip to America? We never got a chance to discuss it the other night. I must tell you though, I do believe the bad-uns knew you had left town."

I was rather surprised by Lestrade's admission. Holmes, however, was his usual nonchalant self and ignored the compliment, saying only, "I'm certain the name Lestrade is uttered with an equal degree of trepidation by those same 'bad-uns.'"

I was even more taken aback by Holmes' praise of Lestrade, but the inspector seemed touched, saying only, "I do hope you are right, but I rather doubt it."

"I shall be in touch if I learn anything, Lestrade."

"Thank you, Mr. Holmes, and try not to pull any more lengthy disappearing acts, will you?"

With that, he rose and let himself out. After I had heard the door close, I said, "Holmes, you are incorrigible."

"Lestrade is up against it, Watson. I thought he could use a little encouragement. Besides, we *are* going to disappear again, and I will not be able to assist him with his case – even though he may have greatly aided me with my investigation."

"Did that stone tell you something?"

"Take a look, and tell me what you see," he said handing me the stone and his lens.

The stone was perhaps two inches long by one-and-a-half wide and maybe a quarter of an inch thick. It weighed about an ounce. Although the primary color was green, there were thin flecks of white and grey throughout. I examined it carefully but could discern nothing. I looked at Holmes and said ruefully, "Its meaning escapes me."

"It's what's called a 'worry stone.' They can trace their origins to ancient Greece. They are also used by the natives of Tibet as well as a number of Native American tribes, and, of course, people in Ireland. They are, in fact, quite common. However, unless I miss my guess this one has been fashioned from Connemara marble. Sometimes called 'Irish green,' it is a rare variety of marble found only in Connemara in County Galway on the west coast of Ireland. It has a distinctive green hue and is often used for jewelry and decoration. Due to its colouration, one finds it frequently associated with the Irish."

"Holmes, you amaze me, but why didn't you share that information with Lestrade?"

"We are dealing with Irish terrorists sorely in need of funds, and a piece of distinctive Irish stone shows up in the midst of a spate of high-end thefts. I don't think even you would believe that is a coincidence, and the last thing I need right now is Lestrade blundering about in the middle of my investigation."

"You think the Fenians are behind the thefts?"

"I think something delayed the money Michael was expecting from America, and since he knows he will have to pay me tomorrow night, he has turned to theft to make up the shortfall."

"And why was the right or left so important?"

"As I am sure you have noticed, Jimmy is left-handed, and he constantly has his hand in his coat pocket. Now, let us enjoy the rest of our evening. I expect we have a long day in front of us tomorrow." With that he took his violin from its case and began to play. I did not recognize the piece and began to suspect that it was a composition of his own.

The next morning we rose early, donned our workman's attire and left through the tradesmen's entrance while it was still quite dark. After a day on the docks, we dined at a pub and then made our way to the Ten Bells. Michael was waiting for us at his usual table. As we sat down, he said, "You certainly know how to disappear when you want to."

"I've had some practice," Holmes said amiably. "Were you looking for me?"

Ignoring Holmes' question, Michael said, "Do you have a list for me?"

"Only if you have money for me."

Michael nodded and Jimmy slid an envelope across the table. As Holmes reached for it, Michael said, "There's £200 in small notes to cover your expenses for the explosives and the timers. I'll expect receipts and money back. Now, my list."

With that, Holmes withdrew a sheet of paper from his jacket pocket and handed it to Michael. He looked it over, smiling as he did so. "Aye, now we're talkin'. I have to say that's a rather ambitious undertaking and quite specific. Second row of bookshelves on the right side of the Reading Room in the London Library. Under the third display case in the middle of the Egyptian exhibit at the British Museum. Can you really do all this?"

"Pick the ones you like and I'll make it 'appen."

"I thought you were going to give me a list of 30 targets – there's only 20 here."

"If I recall, you first said 15 and then you suddenly changed it to 30 because you were afraid we might disagree on some. Tell me the ones you don't like. There are five extra, after all."

Michael sat there searching for words when Holmes suddenly turned to me and said, "Ya know wat I t'ink, Hamish? I t'ink Michael wanted me to scout out some targets for his other bomb-maker. I t'ink he was tryin' to get us to work fer free."

Michael's face turned as red as his ginger hair. Through clenched teeth, he said only, "How much?"

"For what?" replied Holmes, the very picture of innocence.

"The other list of targets."

Holmes smiled, "I think 10 quid should cover it."

Michael reached into his pocket and came out with another note which he handed to Holmes. While he was doing that, Holmes was withdrawing the second sheet of paper from his pocket and handing it to Michael.

After perusing it, Michael looked at Holmes and said, "There is quite a difference between these targets and those on the first list you gave me. These are not nearly as specific."

Holmes replied, "My list is based on my reconnaissance. I have visited each locale – often more than once – and I know exactly where I want to place to the bomb so that it will have its greatest effect. Your other bomb-maker has got to make his own observations and see where he thinks the bombs will be most effective, what time they should be detonated and all that."

"Wouldn't you and he come to the same conclusion?" asked Jimmy.

"Placing a bomb – just like making a bomb – requires a certain degree of skill. Different bomb-makers may arrive at the same conclusion, but they may also differ significantly. Your campaign has been largely ineffective thus far because you seem to have chosen your targets willy-nilly. Mix bad target selection with poorly made bombs and you've got a recipe for disaster. I think even you will admit, your campaign has had more misses than hits to date."

"I'll confess we could've done better," said Michael.

"I have taken great pains in arranging *my* list of targets. I know exactly where I'll place the explosive and when. I know the best time for detonation. My bombs will not only explode – they will terrorize.

"I'd suggest you either impress upon your other bomb-maker the importance of planning – I say that because presumably he doesn't know London – or you let me teach him my methods."

"You do make a point," Michael said. "But, you've got to understand my position – I need to keep things and people separate. If the peelers nick you, you might give up me and Jimmy and a few others but no more. Why? Because I've deliberately kept you and Hamish separate from most of the rest of my group. By the same token, there are any number of other members, who don't even know you two exist.

"Safety is a two-way street, Mr. Fergus. If you knew the identity of my other bomber, who knows what that information might be worth to Scotland Yard.

"No, Mr. Fergus, I'll take your suggestion under advisement and see if there isn't some way to impart your methods to my new bomb-maker. Of course, there is always a chance that you might learn a thing or two – were you ever to meet."

"I am always a willing student," replied Holmes. "Now, we're off. Lots to do tomorrow getting supplies all over London."

"I'm busy tomorrow night myself," added Michael. "Shall we meet again in two nights' time?"

"At eight, here?"

"Yes."

"We'll see you then." As we neared the door, Michael called out, "Don't forget the receipts."

Holmes merely waved, and then we were in the street. After a few steps, Holmes stopped to retie his bootlace.

As we walked along, I looked behind us to make certain no one was following or in earshot and then I said, "Well, that seems to have gone pretty well."

Holmes also looked back before replying, "Better than I might have hoped. Did you see Wiggins anywhere?"

"No, why?"

"He was hiding in the shadows of the house across the street from the Ten Bells. I must say he's getting quite good at blending into his surroundings."

When we arrived at the flat, I was exhausted, but Holmes sat up reading and smoking. As I was preparing to turn in, he said, "Did you happen to notice Jimmy's left coat pocket?"

I had completely forgot and admitted my shortcoming.

"It was definitely repaired in the last week or two and by someone who is not a seamstress."

"So they were involved in the thefts?"

"It would appear so. Now, good night, Watson."

At first I thought it was a dream, but then I woke as I heard a light rapping at the door. Holmes let Wiggins in and whispered, "What's the news, boy?"

"I'm awake," I said. "No need to whisper."

"Go on, Wiggins. You were saying."

"Somethin' queer 'appened after you and Dr. Watson left."

"Be precise and tell me everything you saw and heard."

"The pub closed at midnight, but Michael didn't come out right away. I waited another 'our and then a wagon pulls up. Michael comes out and says to the driver, 'Just be a minute.' Then he goes back inside and a few minutes later, him and another fella roll out a full barrel of beer and load it onto the truck."

"How do you know it was full?"

"The two of 'em was strugglin' somethin' awful to lift it into the wagon bed. It 'ad to be full. After they got it loaded, Michael says to the driver, 'You know wat to do.' And then he turned to his friend wat helped him load it and said something, but I din't understand it at all. Seemed like 'e was just makin' a bunch o' noises."

"Can you recall the sounds at all?" asked Holmes.

Wiggins made an effort to repeat what he had heard. "It sounded like '*Féach leat oiche amárach*.' Is it a secret code, Mr. 'Olmes?"

Holmes chuckled, "No, my boy, he was merely saying, 'See you tomorrow night' in his native language."

Wiggins seemed nonplussed, "I don't understand. Isn't English his native language? I've heard 'im speak it."

"No, Wiggins, Irish is his native language, but he also speaks English."

"So he speaks two languages?"

I could see the thought of learning two tongues had overwhelmed the boy.

"Perhaps more," replied Holmes. "Was anyone able to follow the wagon?"

"I'm sorry, Mr. 'Olmes. I was by meself tonight, and I stuck with Michael, who went right home."

"Was there anything distinctive about the wagon?"

"About the wagon, no. But the driver was quite tall and very thin and he wore a red watch cap. The 'orse was a dapple gray wif a plaited tail."

"Wiggins, you are getting quite good at this. Now, I want you and the other Irregulars to keep following Michael. And you can continue to report here to me. If anything out of the ordinary happens, open the front door and put a small mark near the bottom hinge with a piece of chalk. Can you remember that? And if it's urgent, mark a small 'X.'"

"Got it, Mr. Holmes." With that he was out the door.

"What do you make of it, Holmes?"

"I'm not certain, Watson, but it does bear looking into. The horse and driver should be easily found. They are probably based somewhere in the area."

"Why do you say that?"

"Because Michael spoke to him in English."

"And what made Wiggins come here at this hour?"

"I told him I wanted to see him as soon as possible?"

"When? You've been with me all day. When did you have time to see Wiggins?"

With that Holmes bent and tied his bootlace. He smiled up at me and said, "It's a prearranged signal we have."

"So what's our next move, Holmes?"

"I think it is imperative that we learn what was in that barrel. If Michael has that much gunpowder, he could be up to all kinds of mischief."

Chapter 11

The next day was sunny and warmer, and it seemed an auspicious omen. Holmes had tasked me with learning the whereabouts of the wagon drawn by the dappled grey. Bright and early I set out planning to visit every livery stable in the area, but the grey horse and tall driver remained as elusive as our unknown bomb-maker. After a long and frustrating day, I returned to the flat early in the evening to find Holmes sitting in front of the fire smoking his pipe. He scarcely took notice of my entrance, and not knowing what state of mind he might be in, I refrained from any attempt at conversation.

Finally, after about ten minutes, he turned to me and said, "I can see you have had no luck." Then after a pause, he continued, "This problem has proven far more vexing than I had first anticipated." Before I could reply, he continued, "We know almost everything we need to know, but the one piece of information – the identity of the other bomb-maker – continues to elude us."

"You have made yourself invaluable to them; I am certain it is just a matter of time before someone lets something slip."

"I am not certain we can wait for that, old man. After all, in the presence of strangers, which we still are to a degree, they remain a rather laconic bunch."

"That's the god's honest truth."

"Still, I have one more card to play."

"Do you?" I inquired. "Do tell."

With that Holmes turned to me and a sort of half-smile of satisfaction crossed his face. It was a look I had become familiar with, and it never boded well for me. "Holmes," I said, "I have already given up a comfortable life. I'm a physician posing as a dockworker, and the days of decent meals and a comfortable bed seem like little more than a distant memory. What else would you have me do?"

With that he began to outline his plan to me, and although I wasn't looking forward to it, I could certainly see the logic behind it. After he had finished, I said simply, "When would you like me to start?"

"There's no time like the present," he replied.

"And what will you be doing while I'm out?"

"Building timers," he replied, "but first I must do some shopping."

We left together, and Holmes went his way while I headed towards the Ten Bells. I entered and saw Jimmy and two other fellows sitting in the back. I waved and Jimmy beckoned me over. As I approached the table, he asked, "Where's your partner?"

"He's doing some rather sensitive work," I replied with a knowing wink, "and he prefers to work in silence, so I decided to get myself a pint."

"Better him acting the maggot with that stuff than me," said Jimmy. I nodded and said, "I totally agree."

"Considerin' what he does, I suppose I ken understand him bein' all about the dough. Still, as you ken see, it don't sit right with Michael." He then introduced me to his two companions, Declan and Charlie. Both were husky and tall, one might call

109

them strapping, and I am certain they would acquit themselves well in any type of brawl.

"They're good lads and loyal to the cause."

We continued chatting, and after about twenty minutes, I decided to broach the subject, "Where is Michael tonight?"

Jimmy looked about and in a low voice answered vaguely, "He's meetin' someone." Deciding that pursuing the subject would only arouse suspicion, I dropped it, and we began talking about the turf and other anodyne subjects. I listened to every word the men said and they gave nothing away – even after I had stood them to a few rounds.

Finally, around ten o'clock, I gave up, wished them goodnight and headed back to the flat. I let myself in quietly in order not to disturb Holmes, but I needn't have bothered as he was nowhere to be found. On the table, I discovered a note with a few words in Holmes' spidery script.

I will probably be quite late.

Not knowing what the morrow would bring, I decided to turn in. Perhaps it was the ale, but I must say that I slept soundly and when I awoke in the morning, I saw Holmes sitting at the table, seemingly deep in thought.

He looked up and said, "Ah, you are finally awake. It's just six, old man, and we have quite a few things to do today."

"I don't suppose it would do any good to ask what you were up to last night."

Holmes ignored my implied question, and answered with a query of his own. "Did you learn anything from the fellows at the pub?"

"Only that they are quite tight-lipped – even when they are drinking. Michael wasn't there, so I was hoping a few pints might loosen their tongues but to no avail."

"Yes, Michael was indisposed last evening."

"Indisposed? Is he ill?"

Holmes laughed, "Not at all, Watson. He spent the night in the company of a woman. Tall, slender, auburn hair, mid-thirties, I should guess. I am certain you would find her quite attractive.

"After a late supper at F Cooke's on Hoxton Street, a meal they lingered over for an inordinate amount of time I might add, he escorted her back to her room on Blossom Street; he then went straight home to Folgate Street. I waited an hour in case he ventured out again, then I returned here and found you sleeping quite soundly."

"I thought you were going to spend the evening building timers."

"I fully intended to, but when Wiggins made his report, I decided to spend some time looking in on Michael myself."

"Suppose he had seen you?"

"I went disguised as a bobby. Truth be told, we passed each other on the pavement and he wished me a good evening."

"Holmes, you are taking more risks than is your usual wont."

"We know what they are planning, Watson. I am merely attempting to ascertain whether I might serve as a catalyst in some way."

"You don't think that the woman could be the other bomber?"

"I'll admit the thought had crossed my mind, but she seemed a lady of some breeding, so I am inclined to disregard that notion. Besides, I think Michael is quite smitten with her."

"Perhaps, she has some connection to the other bomber – wife? Sister?"

"It's possible but unlikely, I think."

"Did you ever do the shopping you intended to last night?"

"Unfortunately, no. Wiggins arrived shortly after you left, so I must be about that business today."

"Would you like some company?"

"I think not. I want you to go to the docks and work your shift. I shall meet you at the Ten Bells at seven for supper."

I did as Holmes instructed, and after apologizing for my tardiness and being told my pay would be docked, I spent the rest of the day unloading untold crates of coffee. After work I headed for the Ten Bells. I arrived perhaps twenty minutes early and took a seat at one of the rear tables. I saw Jimmy enter perhaps ten minutes later and gave him a friendly wave which he reciprocated.

A few minutes after that Holmes entered and joined me. We ordered pints and two bowls of stew. After we had finished and were leaving, Holmes sidled up to Jimmy at the bar. "Where's Michael?"

"He's about somewhere," replied Jimmy.

"When you see him, tell him to meet us here tomorrow at eight. I've got some important news to share with him."

"You can tell me. I'll make sure he gets the message."

Holmes merely replied, "I think not. Tomorrow night at eight."

With that he turned on his heel and left. When I caught up to him I said, "Are you trying to make an enemy of Jimmy?"

"Not exactly. I'm just hoping to sow a bit of dissension in the ranks."

"Well, I am inclined to think you are succeeding."

When we arrived home, Holmes knocked on the door of the flat shared by Jenny and her sister, Julie. It was Julie who opened the door. "May I have that box back now?" he asked.

She asked us to wait a minute and returned carrying a wooden chest, perhaps a foot square and five or six inches deep. Holmes thanked her and handed the girl a few coins. She tried to refuse but he insisted. "I'll be bringing it back in a bit," he informed her.

When we had entered our flat, he placed the chest on the table, withdrew a small key from his vest pocket and unlocked it. After fiddling with it for another minute or two, he lifted out a tray filled with spools of thread, a few pin cushions, a tape measure and other sewing paraphernalia. That was followed by more fiddling and the removal of a second tray similar to the first.

"What have you got there, Holmes? And why are you entrusting it to those young ladies?"

After he had placed the second tray on the table, he reached into the box and withdrew a small item wrapped in gauze from the very bottom of the chest. After removing the cloth, he held up a small metal tube, perhaps two inches long, and said, "Have you any idea what this is?"

"Not the slightest."

"It's the latest type of blasting cap, and I have twenty of them here."

"Are you really going to use them in bombs?"

"Oh heavens, no," he replied. "But these will go a long way towards burnishing my bona fides with the Fenians. The biggest problems with their bombs in the past were caused by the detonators. For example, in one bomb, they used an alarm clock that had been wired to a small pistol. The gun was aimed at a brick of Atlas powder. As time passed, the wire attached to the trigger tightened. Fortunately, the gun misfired.

"In another bomb, they used sulphuric acid, which they poured over wool. The acid eventually worked its way through the wool to the detonator and the bomb exploded. However, as you can see, it's a fairly inexact science in their hands. They have seen one 'demonstration' of my abilities. I am hoping that these detonators which are far more precise than anything they have tried will prove too enticing to resist."

"Suppose they were to get their hands on those? Wouldn't all London be in danger?"

"Come, come, Watson. I may take the occasional risk, but I am not foolhardy. Only three of these detonators will actually work. Instead of black powder, the others have been filled with inert material."

"I see," I said, still not totally understanding why Holmes was doing this.

"Why are you storing them with the sisters?"

"There is no good place to hide them here. So should anyone decide to search our rooms while we are out, there is nothing to find. I have instructed the sisters to keep the chest hidden and to be quite careful when handling it."

"Are they in any danger, Holmes?"

"Not as long as they follow my instructions."

"I can't say that I approve."

"I am not fond of involving innocent outsiders either, but to paraphrase Hippocrates, 'Desperate times call for desperate measures.'"

Holmes then removed two detonators from the box and after replacing the tray and locking it, he returned it to Jenny when she answered the door.

Upon returning to the flat, he placed the two detonators in two different pockets of his coat. "Now let us get some rest. Unless I miss my guess, tomorrow may prove to be another busy day."

In the morning, we rose, ate a meager breakfast, and set out for the docks. As we neared the gate, I heard a voice cry out, "Oy, Fergus."

Turning around, I saw Jimmy trotting towards us. "Michael wants to see you right now."

Holmes started to object, but before he could finish his thought, Jimmy interrupted him, saying, "And before you ask, he says he'll give you a day's wages for wat you'll lose at the docks. Best of all, he says he'll only need you fer 'alf a day."

We then followed Jimmy as he led us to the basement on Turner Street. We descended the few stairs into the low-ceilinged room which seemed even smaller and closer in the daylight. Michael was sitting at the table with a candle in the middle. "What's this all about?" demanded Holmes.

115

"And top o' the mornin' to you too, Mr. Fergus," Michael replied with a broad smile on his face. "And you as well, Hamish."

"Why have you summoned us here so early?" Holmes demanded.

"So, today you are all business. Well, then, we've been dancin' this dance for several weeks now, and it occurred to me I have yet to see you in action myself. I thought you might give me a small demonstration, so that I ken decide whether to continue dancin' or seek another partner."

"You want me to blow somethin' up this mornin'?" asked Holmes incredulously.

"That sums it up nicely."

"That's not how I work," replied Holmes. "I told you before, these things require planning. You need to know where the coppers are, the timing of their patrols, and a hundred other things."

"So what you're sayin' then is that when it comes to bombs, you are an artiste?"

"I never said that."

"No, but you certainly implied it, and your bearing underscores that notion. Look, all I want this mornin' is to see somethin' blown up. Is that too much to ask?

"Also, I shouldn't have to remind you that you work fer me, so let's get to it, shall we?"

"Do you have the materials I'll need?"

"Aye, that I do," replied Michael and with that he hoisted a bag from the floor to the table and then pushed it towards Holmes. I watched as Holmes opened it and removed two sticks of dynamite, an alarm clock, some wool, a bottle of liquid and another contraption – the likes of which I had never seen before.

"You canna be serious!" stated Holmes. "Where's the detonator?"

"Use the wool and sulphuric acid. It's worked for us before."

"Why don't you just light a long fuse and hope fer the best?" asked Holmes sarcastically.

"What would you suggest?"

"I need some tools – pliers, hammer, saw – as well as a small metal tube, an eight-inch piece of safety fuse and that battery you have there."

"Fer wat?" asked Michael.

"I'll make me own detonator if ya don't mind – wool and acid," he shook his head and laughed bitterly.

"And where would you like us to get those things at this time o' day?" asked Jimmy.

"I have everyt'ing I need in me flat. Hamish will stay with you, and I'll be back as soon as I ken."

"Jimmy, you'll go with Mr. Fergus," said Michael.

"He'll just slow me down."

"He'll go just the same."

Michael and I said little over the course of the next hour. When Holmes and Jimmy finally returned, Holmes was carrying a small sack. "I have everythin' I need right here. Now would you like to watch me work or would you prefer to wait outside?"

"Why would we do that?" asked Jimmy.

"Accidents do happen," laughed Holmes, holding up his the backs of his hands towards us with the fingers bent down towards him as if he had lost all his fingers. "In this space, we'd all be blown to kingdom come. Yer welcome to stay, but I'm jus' tryin' to give yer fair warnin'."

With those words, we started to leave, but Holmes said, "Hamish, I'll be needin' your assistance."

When we were alone, he began to assemble the bomb. "Watch carefully," he said in a low voice. "Taking them apart is easy. This way if I'm not there, you'll be able to disarm one by yourself." I watched as he inserted the blasting cap into the dynamite. He then wrapped strips of fabric around the two sticks, and then he secured the fabric with rubber adhesive. Finally he attached the alarm clock and the battery.

"If you want to disarm the bomb," he said, "the easiest thing is to pull the blasting cap from the dynamite. Still, be careful, blasting caps are small explosives and they can be set off in various ways."

"How were you able to procure these things, with Jimmy accompanying you?"

"I made him wait outside. I told him to keep an eye out for coppers. It was fortunate I decided to keep two detonators in my coat; otherwise, I might have had to involve Julie or Jenny – something I am trying desperately to avoid."

"What are you going to do with this bomb? Michael is demanding a demonstration."

"And he shall have one. I anticipated this moment and have planned for it accordingly."

Suddenly we heard Michael's voice. "We're wastin' time, and I don't have all day. I have other pressing matters that require my attention."

"Just a few more minutes," replied Holmes. After he had packed everything in a small Gladstone, we emerged from the basement. Holmes held up the bag, "What exactly would you like this bomb to do?"

"Since it's your special detonator, I'd like you to tell me when it's going to explode, and then I'd like to see it explode at that time. Is that too much to ask?"

"Not at all, not at all. Is there somethin' special you want blown up because it's not a very powerful bomb."

"It's two sticks of dynamite. Whaddaya mean it's not powerful?" asked Jimmy.

Holmes wheeled on him, "Your ignorance is showin', lad."

Jimmy made a move towards Holmes, but Michael stepped between them. "If it's not too much trouble, perhaps you'd care to explain yourself, Mr. Fergus."

"How old is the dynamite? Has it been stored in a dry place? Has the dynamite wept at all? You see, Jimmy, there's a lot you've yet to learn about dynamite. I'm guessin' by the looks of it that some of the nitroglycerine has been lost. Unless, of course, you can tell me otherwise."

Holmes looked at Jimmy but no answer was forthcoming. "At 10 Downing Street, I used my dynamite, and I knew its history. All I can do here is hope."

Turning to Michael, Holmes said, "You have a decision to make. I can place it at one of the targets on my list, and we can wait and see what, if anything, happens."

"What's my other option?" asked Michael.

"We take it someplace, and I give you exactly what you asked for – a demonstration. Since I'm placing the bomb, and since I haven't reconnoitered any specific targets for this morning, I'd suggest we choose a place that's open and provides us with ready escape routes. But as you've reminded me, you're the boss."

"It's comin' up on half seven. I know where I want to go, and I do want to see you in action. There'll be no need for reconnaissance. We're just goin' to make a statement of sorts to an old friend," said Michael. With that, he turned to Jimmy and said, "Why don't you see if you can find us a cab, lad?"

About twenty minutes later, Jimmy said, "I've got one waitin' on Stepney Way." We walked to the cab and fortunately, or perhaps by design, it was a growler. Michael spoke to the driver, but I couldn't hear what he said. We then set off at a slow canter, and little was said during the journey.

I watched as the city slowly came to life on that brisk April morning. I saw shopkeepers sweeping their walks, costermongers hawking their wares and youngsters on their way to school – all blissfully ignorant of the danger passing them by. I also wondered what sort of test awaited us. For most of the journey we were never too far from the Thames. After about forty minutes, we left the Embankment and drove past the equestrian statue of Charles I, and I knew we weren't too far from Great Scotland Yard. A few minutes later we passed the gates of Buckingham Palace. I had no idea what our destination was, but I had decided that Michael must be insane.

I looked over at Holmes, but he was sitting in silence, his eyes half-closed, cradling the Gladstone in his lap. We finally descended from the cab on Belgrave Place at Eton Square Gardens. "I trust you know where we are," said Michael.

"I don't normally come to this part of town, but if I had to guess, I'd say Belgravia," ventured Holmes.

"Righto, Mr. Fergus." Pointing whence we had come, he said, "We just passed Eccleston Mews and prior to that is Eaton Place. I want you to walk to Eaton Place and turn right. Then I want you to deposit your bag in front of the second house on the side of the street closest to us. I want your bomb to detonate five minutes after that. Do you understand?"

"I do. Do you want part of the house destroyed or do you just want to scare the people inside?"

"I'll leave that to you Mr. Fergus."

"Whose house is it?"

"A bloody bastard's," exclaimed Jimmy with an unexpected degree of venom.

Maintaining his composure, Michael replied, "The house belongs to Sir Charles Trevelyan. I trust that name is familiar to you."

"'Tis indeed," replied Holmes, who then uttered an oath of his own.

"He's an old man now, and so far he's escaped punishment for his sins against our people. Perhaps this is some small measure of recompense. If you can find a way to detonate the bomb inside the house, so much the better."

"Count on me, guv," said Holmes, as he lifted the Gladstone and strolled back up Belgrave Place. He looked like any other tradesman on his way to a job. I watched as he turned in at Eaton Place. Some four or five minutes later he reappeared and began walking towards us at a leisurely pace. When he finally rejoined us, he said, "You know there is a bit of guesswork involved here."

"Guesswork?" roared Michael. "I'm not paying for guesswork. I'm paying for precision."

"Well if you want things to go off exactly, you're going to have to buy me a watch. It's difficult to tell time without one. Still, by my guess, it shouldn't be more than another…"

Suddenly, we heard a loud explosion that rocked the neighborhood. I heard glass shattering in the distance and women screaming, and Holmes continued as though nothing had happened, "…second or two."

Chapter 12

"Well done, Mr. Fergus," exclaimed Michael, clapping Holmes on the back as we walked toward Elizabeth Street in search of another growler. There were a million questions I wanted to ask Holmes, but I remained silent. Finally, Jimmy was able to secure a cab and despite our disreputable appearance, the driver agreed to take us as far as Leman Street – provided we paid half the fare in advance.

We spent the ride conversing in low tones about how Trevelyan deserved what had just happened and "a great deal more," according to both Jimmy and Michael.

"We've had our differences, but sure, 'tis a grand ting you've done on this fine April mornin', Mr. Fergus, and I apologize fer ever doubtin' yer ability," said Jimmy.

Michael was less effusive in his praise but still seemed duly impressed with the smoothness with which Holmes had operated and his grace under pressure. "I always suspected you were a cool one, and now I know fer certain."

When we arrived at the Ten Bells, Michael told the publican, "A bottle of yer best whiskey."

"Scotch or Irish?"

"I'm goin to ferget you asked that question, you silly sod."

We took our usual table in the back, and the barman soon brought us a tray with four glasses. He returned a moment later and placed a bottle of Bushmills on the table.

He then left us, and Michael poured each of us a rather substantial drink. He then toasted Fergus, freedom and those who sacrificed all in the fight for liberty. Although it was not quite ten o'clock, I felt obliged to join in the celebration even though it was against my better judgment.

After a second round had been consumed and a third poured, Michael said, "Down to business then."

"Finally," said Holmes.

"I'm told a case of blasting caps went missing from the Hyde Park Barracks. You wouldn't happen to know anyt'ing about that would you, Mr. Fergus?"

"I might," said Holmes.

"How much?" asked Michael.

"I'm told there were twenty in the box. I imagine one might have got lost somewhere, so if, and I'm only sayin' if, I could lay me hands on 'em, I could let you have 'em for twenty quid."

"Done," said Michael. "The one that got lost, you didn't by chance see it this morning did ya?"

"I might have," laughed Holmes, and both Michael and Jimmy laughed with him.

"You are a shrewd one, Mr. Fergus, but if you can pull this off to my specifications, you'll have been worth all the aggravation – and every blessed pound." With that he laughed again, proceeded to top off everyone's glass, and offered a toast, "To liberty, justice and Ireland."

I had been deliberately nursing my drink, taking only small sips, and my reluctance had not gone unnoticed. "Not much of a drinker, are you, Hamish?" asked Jimmy.

Thinking of my brother, I replied truthfully, "'Tis the curse of my family."

I was surprised when Michael said, "Mine as well, so I understand your reluctance."

"When do you want to start your campaign?" asked Holmes.

Michael looked at him and said, "You're so clever, why don't you tell me."

"I'm tinkin' with May fast approaching, you'll be wanting to wish everybody in London a very happy May Day."

"Cool and bright," said Michael. "The first of May is also the ancient feast of Beltaine or *Lá Bealtaine*. I'd like to hope that this May ushers in a summer that will go down in history. Can you have everyt'ing ready by then?"

"I can, but what about the other dynamiter?"

"You just make your bombs and worry about your list. I'll see to the rest if you don't mind."

"When will you be wantin' all the bombs?"

"I'd like to have everyt'ing in my hands by April 28th. That gives you a little less than two weeks. We will meet the next day to coordinate and make final plans, and then the fun begins on the morning of the 1st. Oh, it'll be a grand day fer sure."

We then had another drink, and I knew I had to stop. When we left the pub a while later, I wanted nothing more than some solid food and a chance to talk about the day's events with Holmes.

We arrived home and when we opened the front door, I spotted a small X in chalk by the bottom hinge.

"Wiggins has been here."

"I see that," said Holmes, "and the 'X' tells me it's important."

No sooner had we entered the hall than we were greeted by Jenny. "The boy who visits you from time to time was here again this morning. He came not five minutes after you left. He did slip a note under your door. He told me if I saw you to tell you it was urgent."

Holmes thanked her, and we went inside. He snatched up the note and read it. "What does it say, Holmes?"

"Wiggins says he has important information for me. I'm to meet him at Baker Street at five o'clock."

"Excellent! I could do with one of Mrs. Hudson's suppers."

"I'm afraid you'll have to remain here, Watson. With all that's going on, you never know who might stop by. If I can, I'll bring something back for you."

"Before I agree to anything, you must tell me what happened this morning? Was anyone hurt? Was there much damage?"

Holmes smiled. "I rang the bell at Trevelyan's house, but no one answered. So I placed the bomb under his steps and stayed as long as I could to make certain no one was nearby."

"We've been very lucky so far, Holmes. What would you have done, had anyone been home?"

"Again, luck has had nothing to do with it. If you recall, Trevelyan was the man responsible for Michael's father losing his farm. So I took the liberty of contacting Robert Orr and suggesting Trevelyan's health might be better served were he to

126

spend some time at his estate in Wallington – under police guard, of course."

"Holmes, you never fail to amaze me. How many other men have they marked for death, do you suppose?"

"That's impossible to say, but from what I have been able to glean, Trevelyan was considered the worst malefactor – and I suppose with good reason – in their eyes.

"Now, Watson, take that nap you so desperately need. Drinking before noon doesn't appear to agree with you. I will wake you before I leave."

I was tempted to protest, but I was feeling rather lethargic and decided that a brief nap would do me more good than a prolonged argument. At around four o'clock, Holmes woke me and said, "I don't think I'll be late."

After he had stepped out the door, I was torn between foraging for food and resuming my nap. Hoping that Holmes wouldn't forget his promise, I decided to go back to sleep, and within minutes I was dead to the world.

Sometime later, I felt someone shaking me and I heard Holmes' voice telling me, "Wake up." After a few minutes, I was fully awake but as I stretched, I could see Holmes smiling, "And you call me incorrigible." With that he threw a newspaper on the table.

"What's the news, Holmes?"

"The papers all covered the Eaton Place bombing, and I should have to think Michael will be pleased since they attributed it to the Irish Republican Brotherhood."

"I imagine so, but what was so important that Wiggins had to see you?"

"Mrs. Hudson had flagged him down. I have the Irregulars check with her every day. She told Wiggins it was imperative that I visit her at Baker Street as soon as possible."

"And what did she have to say?"

"Mr. Orr stopped by with a letter for me."

"I assume it was a matter of some importance."

"I should think so. They have lost contact with the best of their informants in one of the Brotherhood groups. They haven't heard from him, and no one has seen him in several days now. According to Orr, the man has simply 'disappeared.'"

"But people don't just disappear."

"Exactly."

"So what do you think it means?"

"Do you remember that barrel Wiggins saw Michael and Jimmy load onto a wagon a few nights ago?"

"How could I not? I spent the next day looking for the driver and a grey horse with a plaited tail."

"Originally I thought that the barrel contained black powder, but now I'm wondering if it might have contained something else."

"You don't mean ..."

"That's exactly what I mean. It's certainly one way to get rid of a body. Given your inability to find the driver, I do believe I am onto something."

"But you said you thought he must be local."

"That's when I believed the barrel contained black powder. Now, that I suspect it contained something else, it stands to reason they would employ a driver who isn't known here. They'd want that barrel as far away from here as possible. Since we have no idea in which direction he headed, he could have left the barrel anywhere he wanted on his way home or brought it home and disposed of it there."

"So what's our next move?"

"I'll have the Irregulars scour London in search of the driver and horse. I am not optimistic, but I can't afford to leave any stone unturned. You and I will continue as we have. We will work on the docks during the day, and I'll construct bombs in the evening."

"You're not going to bring more dynamite in here? What about the safety of those charming young women – Jenny and Julie? What about the other tenants? One misstep ..."

Holmes cut me off. "I'll be building the bombs at another of my bolt holes, and if it will ease your conscience, you may rest assured that I will take every precaution possible."

I wasn't totally happy with Holmes' response, but all I could muster was a half-hearted, "Well, thank God for that."

Holmes was as good as his word. The next day we worked unloading a ship laden with goods from South America. After eating supper at a public house, I went back to the flat while Holmes headed off in the general direction of Shadwell and Limehouse. I spent the evening reading. Although I was sorely tempted to write, I refrained on the off-chance that unexpected visitors might drop by or that the flat would be searched again.

That became our routine for the next ten days. One night, having grown tired of staying in, I ventured out to The White Hart. I had no desire to socialize with a group of men who were engaged in such nefarious activities, and I always worried that my face might give me away.

As I was nearing the front door of the public house, I saw a youngster named Grogan, whom I recognized as one of the Irregulars approaching from the opposite direction. I was uncertain whether to greet him, but in an abundance of caution I refrained. I also thought the youngster wouldn't recognize me with my beard and dressed as I was, However, as we passed, he bumped into me and when he turned to apologize, he gave me a knowing wink but otherwise remained silent.

I wondered what the lad might be up to, and decided to broach the subject to Holmes when next I saw him.

After two pints, I decided to head back to the flat. I had just stepped onto the pavement when I heard a familiar voice say, "Wat's the matter? Don't you like drinkin' with us anymore?"

I turned to find Jimmy and another fellow, whose name I believed was Colm, on the sidewalk. "No, not at all. Nothing like that. I was supposed to meet an old friend here."

"Were ya now? Cause you were in there the better part of an hour – and drinkin' alone."

Deciding to seize the initiative, I said, "Why are you followin' me?"

Jimmy laughed and said, "We like ta keep a close eye on all our associates, but yer friend, Fergus, keeps givin' us the slip. Why do ya suppose tat is?"

"He has important work to do – for you."

"We just wanted to check on his progress, see if he needed anything," said Colm.

"Michael has a lot invested in that bloke," Jimmy added.

"I don't know how much more proof you need of his loyalty. You were with him at Downing Street and you saw the newspaper accounts of the bombing at Eaton Place."

"Papers have been known to lie," said Colm.

"But Jimmy was with him at Downing Street," I insisted. "And anyway, if you were to follow him and knock on the door and startle him, you might not be able to report back to Michael."

I could see that my words had resonated with Jimmy, and I am certain he was recalling how Holmes had warned them out of the cellar on Turner Street.

"I'll tell Fergus you're lookin' for him as soon as I see him. Do you want him to come to the Ten Bells tonight when he gets home?"

"Nah, t'won't be necessary. But tell him to stop in soon as he can. Michael has somethin' he wants to discuss wif him."

"I'll give him your message."

I then made my way back to the flat, and it was nearly midnight before I heard Holmes' key in the lock. After he had got settled, I told him everything that had happened.

"You did well, Watson. I was aware I was being followed, and I should have suspected they'd start tailing you after they kept losing me."

I then recalled seeing Grogan on the street and recounted that meeting such as it was to Holmes. He chuckled and said, "Grogan was on his way here to tell you I'd be quite late. I'm glad the boy had sense enough not to deliver his message on the street.

"Jimmy gave you no hint as to why Michael wanted to see me?"

"No."

"Well, perhaps in a day or two, we shall drop in at the Ten Bells and beard the lion in his den."

"How goes the bomb-making?"

"My charges are coming along nicely, and then I can begin working on the other half of the batch for the other bomber. It's a painstaking process, trust me."

"Holmes, I know you are doing what you think you must. Still …" and I let the word hang there – more as an invitation than anything else. However, Holmes obviously felt no need to unburden himself to me.

After a rather prolonged silence, he said, "Watson, if you can offer me another course of action, I should be glad to hear it and quite possibly take it. For the present, this is the only way forward I can see."

The next day and evening followed the same pattern; however, when Holmes returned late that night, he informed me his half of the bombs were finally finished. "Tomorrow night we shall make our way to the Ten Bells and see what Michael has to say."

The next night around eight, we entered the pub and saw Michael, Jimmy and two other men, whom I didn't recognize, seated in the rear. We joined them, and after a round had been ordered, Michael said, "You are a smooth one, Mr. Fergus."

"Oh?"

"I had my men try to follow you – you know just to make certain of yer safety – and every night you managed to elude them. Why would you be doin' that?"

"Our arrangement depends upon mutual trust," Holmes replied. "I would think after two demonstrations, I have earned yours but that appears not to be the case."

"I trust you," said Michael.

"If you did, you wouldna have your men followin' me."

"As I said, it's fer yer own safety."

"Rubbish," replied Holmes. "You've had yer men break into my rooms, steal a stick of dynamite, accompany me on a mission, you've accompanied me on a second mission, and now you're havin' me followed at night. You won't tell me anything about the other dynamiter – which I understand. But all those other t'ings, do they seem like trust to you?"

Michael's face had reddened while Holmes was speaking. I'm certain he was not used to be being rebuked or spoken to in such a manner – at least not in public and certainly not in front of his men.

After a long pause, he said, "Yer right, Mr. Fergus. I find it hard to trust people. We've had any number of informers in our ranks since we formed – betraying their brothers and their country fer a few shillings from the Crown. Some we've turned to our advantage; others we had to deal with in a more straightforward way.

"You have my word that from now on, none of my men will be followin' you or Hamish." And when he extended his hand, Holmes shook it.

As we rose to leave, Michael said, "Just a week until our next meeting. I trust everything will be completed."

"Aye, they will all be finished. Do you want me to bring them here that night or someplace else?"

"I'll tell you when and where to bring the bombs on the morning of the 29th. I know I originally said the 28th which is tomorrow, but that gives you an extra day, if you need it. Speaking of trust, do you have any money or receipts for me?"

Holmes reached into his pocket and extracted a small sheaf of papers and notes which he had secured with an elastic band. He handed them to Michael who put them into his pocket. "Ya see, I'm not even going to count the money or look at the receipts because I trust you, Mr. Fergus."

Holmes nodded in appreciation.

"Just make certain you never let me down or deceive me, and we'll get along just grand! Also you might do well to bear in mind that betrayal of me or the cause has dire consequences. Good night, Mr. Fergus, Hamish. Enjoy the rest of your evening."

Chapter 13

After we had returned to the flat, I said to Holmes, "Michael does not strike me as the type of man who makes idle threats."

"I quite agree, Watson. His parting words were a less-than-subtle warning. So while we have been quite careful thus far, from this point on, we must proceed with even greater caution."

The next morning, I was awakened by the sound of someone knocking on the door. "Who is it?" I yelled.

"It's me," came the reply. Fortunately, I recognized Wiggins' voice, and as I went to let him in, I realized Holmes was not in the flat.

Opening the door, I said, "Do you have any idea what time it is?"

With that Wiggins unbuttoned his coat and produced a silver watch from his waistcoat pocket, opened it and said, "It's exactly four minutes after six."

"Do I want to know how you came by such a handsome timepiece?"

"Probably not," said Wiggins, with a broad grin. "But if you must, a toff dropped it while walking along Marylebone Road."

"Fell out of his pocket, did it?"

"Somethin' like that."

"Wiggins, Holmes needs you. If you get pinched for pickpocketing, his plans could be in jeopardy. Can you refrain until after this case is concluded?"

"I never thought of it that way. I s'pose I'll have to quit for a bit, now won't I?"

While he was mulling it over, I just said, "It's important, Wiggins. We depend on you for so many things." Looking about, I added, "We all have sacrifices to make."

Now it was his turn to survey the rather dismal flat and after some consideration, he concluded, "If you can give up Baker Street – and Mrs. 'Udson's cooking – to live 'ere. I s'pose I can give up pinching for a bit."

About ten minutes later, Holmes returned. As soon as he saw Wiggins, he said, "What's the news, lad?"

"I waited outside the Ten Bells, and shortly after you left, 'e comes out and 'eads towards Blossom Street. Then 'e goes into a boarding house there, stays about thirty-three minutes and then comes out and 'eads back to 'is own crib."

"Thirty-three minutes – that's rather precise. Well done, Wiggins."

"I'm off today. I've got to help me mum. But not to worry Mr. Holmes, I've got two of me best lads watchin' that bloke, and I'll pick him up again tonight."

"Things may be coming to a head soon, Wiggins, so remind the boys to be extra careful. As I told you at the beginning, these are dangerous men."

"No worries, guv." And with that, Wiggins tipped his cap and was out the door.

"Was it a very expensive watch, do you think, Watson?"

"What do you mean, Holmes?"

"The one that Wiggins lifted from some unsuspecting gentleman – did it appear costly?"

"It was a silver hunter and quite dear, I should think. But how on Earth did you know?"

"Although Wiggins is a clever lad, when he told me Michael was in the woman's flat for thirty-three minutes – a rather precise figure, as I mentioned – I can only deduce that he has a timepiece of some sort. His wrists were bare, and since he hadn't rebuttoned his coat I could see the silver watch chain against his waistcoat. I am assuming that you spoke to him about the dangers of his pastime?"

"I did indeed."

"Excellent. When this is all over, I'll examine the watch and see if I can find anything that will lead me to its owner."

"You mustn't say anything to Wiggins, lest he think I was telling tales." Looking at me, Holmes screwed up his face and said in a perfect imitation of the boy's voice, "Wiggins ain't the only one what can pick a pocket."

I had to laugh in spite of myself, and then after recovering, I asked Holmes, "What pressing business has got you up and out so early this morning?"

"I had made arrangements to meet with Lestrade and Smith at a public house near Cambridge Heath. In the broadest possible terms, I indicated that I had become aware of a bombing plot. Smith is going to check with his informants to see if they know anything about the identity of the other bomb-maker."

"I'm sure Lestrade was filled with questions."

"I suppose he was, but I gave him an assignment that should keep him busy, and I also offered a few suggestions about the gang of robbers he is seeking – all designed to lead him further afield and keep him away from Whitechapel."

"You know, Holmes, despite what you perceive as his shortcomings, Lestrade is not stupid."

"True, and while I dislike deceiving the good inspector, I cannot have him toppling the house of cards that I am carefully constructing by suddenly arresting members of Michael's gang for theft – at least not right now. When this is all over, both he and the Yard will be covered in glory – I hope."

"You hope?"

"There are any number of things that are simply beyond my control. Although I try to account for every possible outcome, sometimes that is simply not possible."

At that point I realized the burden under which Holmes had been labouring. In truth he was carrying the safety of the city on his shoulders. Struck hard by my own shortsightedness, I said, "I am certain you will cover yourself in glory as well – even if you and I are the only ones who know it."

He smiled briefly and despite his stoic exterior, I think he was touched by my words.

We then enjoyed breakfast at a nearby public house. We took a seat all the way in the back where Holmes could see the entire room, including the entrance, and where there was little chance of being overheard. As we lingered over a second cup of tea, Holmes said, "We have a few more days before we meet with Michael and just about a week before the first bomb is supposed to go off. With careful planning, I might be able to buy us an extra day, perhaps two, but that will depend upon Michael."

"How on Earth can you forestall the start of the campaign which he so obviously wants to commence on May 1st?"

Holmes then outlined his strategy. When he was near the end, he looked at me and said, "This is what I meant by variables beyond my control. Hopefully, we will not need this particular stratagem, but it's always reassuring to have a contingency plan or two at one's disposal."

As we left the public house, Holmes said, "I want to stroll down Blossom Street to see if I can learn anything more about the woman Michael visits there."

"Would you like some company? I have no plans."

"I think this is better conducted alone, Watson. I'm going to have to visit one of my other bolt-holes and don a new disguise. I don't believe in coincidences, and I'm certain Michael doesn't either. So a change of attire is definitely in order.

"What say we meet at the flat at six, and enjoy a quiet dinner where we won't talk about crime or bombs or Irishmen?"

"Done," I exclaimed.

I watched as Holmes strode off down Sutton Street in the direction of the Thames. With the rest of the day to myself, I considered how I might best use my time. I finally decided the safest thing would be to while away the hours reading, so I headed toward a used bookstore. I was browsing the shelves when I spotted a handsome copy of Henry James' *A Little Tour in France*, a book I had been meaning to read since it had been released the previous year. I was just about to reach for it when it struck me that a man of my station would have no interest in such a book. As a result, I kept on looking and was rewarded when I stumbled across a copy of William Clark Russell's *The Wreck of the Grosvenor*.

I must confess the day flew by so enraptured was I by the rousing tale of Edward Royale and the repugnant officers under whom he served that I was surprised when I heard Holmes' key in the door. I quickly threw the book upon my bed and pulled the cover up over it. When Holmes entered the flat, I was sitting on the bed and asked, "Is it six already?"

"Indeed, it is," he replied. "I hope that during your excursion upon the Atlantic, you have worked up an appetite."

"Holmes how could you possibly know what I've been reading? I hope you aren't having me followed as well."

He laughed, "No, Watson, no one is following you, but if you're going to conceal a book under a blanket, it's best not to sit on the bed lest you pull down the cover and expose the book."

"I shall never get the hang of how you do that."

"There were several other clues that indicated your idleness, but enough of that."

"Well, how was your day? Certainly it was more productive than mine."

"After changing my attire, I made my way to Blossom Street, dressed once again as a bewhiskered constable. I figured if Michael should see me, I would at least be a familiar face. I knocked on the door of the home of Francesca Gerette, an absolutely charming Italian woman, who invited me in for tea.

"I told her there had been a number of thefts in the area and asked if she or any member of her family could recall seeing any strangers in the neighborhood.

"'There are always people coming and going around here,' she said. 'In fact, I have a new tenant who's only been with me a few weeks.'

"I asked, 'Do you think he might have seen anything?'

"She laughed and gently corrected me, 'My tenant is a woman – an Irish woman – Pegeen O'Shea.'

"I asked if she were in, and she informed me Miss O'Shea – for she is indeed single – had gone out early that morning looking for work, and Mrs. Gerette had no idea when she would be back. I asked if that were her only tenant and she informed me she was. She added that she was a very quiet and refined woman – hardly the type I would expect to associate with a firebrand such as Michael.

"Before I left, I thanked her and told her I might stop by another time to talk to Miss O'Shea."

"So what did you learn?"

"Everything seems above board with Miss O'Shea. I have the feeling she's a dead end."

"So then you'll have to look elsewhere for the bomber?"

"It would appear so."

"You had said you didn't suspect the woman, so why go there?"

"As I said, Watson, we are leaving no stone unturned. This case is too important to overlook anything or anyone who might provide a clue."

"Well, we can certainly look for that clue later. If I recall, you promised me a dinner free of talk of bombings, crimes or Irishmen."

"And so I did."

Since we lacked the attire for one of the better restaurants – and as Holmes pointed out there was always the danger of being spotted someplace we didn't belong – we made our way to Narrow Street in Limehouse where we dined on lamb chops with fresh vegetables at The Grapes. It was definitely a welcome respite from the meals we had been eating. Holmes was as good as his word, and for a few hours, it felt as though we were simply enjoying a night out from Baker Street.

The evening was chilly but not unbearably cold, so we decided to walk back to the flat. As we turned into Weyhill Road, I saw two figures standing outside our boarding house. As we drew closer, I recognized Jimmy and the other man who had helped follow me, Colm. I wondered what they might want from us at this late hour.

Before I could say anything, Jimmy strode over to us. "It's about time. Where have you been? We been waitin' here on the pavement for an almost an hour."

"I didn't know we had an appointment, nor that you needed to know our whereabouts at all times."

"Michael wants to see you now – that's all you need to know."

With that he gave a whistle and four more men appeared from the shadows. "No trouble now, ya hear," said Jimmy.

My heart sank in my chest, for I was certain we had been found out. However, Holmes remained his usual implacable self, saying only, "Lead the way."

Chapter 14

After a short walk, we found ourselves at the public house. Although it was not yet ten o'clock, the place was closed. As a result, Jimmy had to knock on the front door. When it was opened, it was obvious the pub was empty. I can't say that I was totally surprised as I deduced this was some sort of emergency meeting.

"Nice of you to join us, Mr. Fergus, and you too, Hamish."

"I wasn't aware that we had a meeting this evening," replied Holmes evenly. "I was under the impression we would next meet on the 29th. That's tomorrow. Nothing was said about a meeting before then."

"Well, that was my original intent," Michael said, "but as I'm sure you're aware, plans change. Sometimes an opportunity falls into your lap, and you have to take advantage of it or spend the rest of your life wondering what might have been. I, for one, refuse to lead a life filled with self-doubt."

"And what's all this got to do with me and Hamish?" Holmes asked.

"I trust you're familiar with the Orange Order."

"If you mean those Protestant bootlickers who are opposed to a free Ireland, I believe I have heard something of them."

"Excellent! Excellent!" exclaimed Michael. "I was certain I could count on you."

"Fer what?"

"I've just learned two prominent Orange Order leaders will be in London tomorrow night to meet with certain members of Parliament the next day. I'd like to make certain that little get-together never takes place."

"You'd like me to build and plant a bomb?"

"And deliver it personally, if you would be so kind."

"I ken build a bomb – and t'at's what you hired me ta do. When it comes to outright killin' that's yer department."

"I'm not certain I follow your objection, Mr. Fergus."

"Let me be blunt then – I'm not an assassin."

"But your bombs have killed people, haven't they?"

"Truth be told, I couldna really say fer certain. However, I can honestly say that I've never built a bomb with the express intention of doin' murder. It may not be much, but it helps me sleep at night.

"So I'll build the bomb – for a price – but get someone else to do your dirty work. Besides, I've got plenty to keep me busy as we prepare for the 1st of May."

"You're a very strange and complicated man, Mr. Fergus. I admire a man with principles, even if their rationale escapes me."

"How big a bomb do ya want? And where's it going?"

"I think two or three sticks should be enough. I'd like the blast to take place in their hotel room tomorrow night, so that they cannot attend any meetings the followin' day. They are staying at the Langham on Portland Place."

"You don't give a fella much time," said Holmes, rubbing his chin thoughtfully. Looking at me, he said, "Do ya t'ink we can pull it off?"

"I t'ink so," I replied.

"It's going to cost yer," said Holmes.

"I thought it would. How much?"

"I t'ink £50 should cover it,"

"Excellent. Can you deliver it here tomorrow night at seven?"

"I'm not sure why ya need to see it. Don't ya trust me anymore?"

Michael ignored Holmes gibe and said, "I like to check everything. I'm a very thorough man. It's what keeps me free and alive. Now do you want the £50, or should I turn it over to someone else? I should not have to remind you, Mr. Fergus, you are no longer the only game in town."

"Don't get yer knickers in a twist," said Holmes lightly. Looking at me, he said, "Finish yer pint. We have werk ta do."

As we walked home I made certain no one was around before I asked, "How are you going to get out of this one?"

"By never getting in it," he replied enigmatically. "Now let me think."

The next morning when I awoke, Holmes was gone. He returned about four in the afternoon and threw himself into his chair. Sensing my apprehension, he said only, "All will be explained in due time."

After a quiet dinner of tinned sardines and bread, we set out for the Ten Bells. We entered the pub at five before the hour and spotted Michael and his cohorts at their usual table. When we sat down, Michael looked at Holmes and said, "I appreciate punctuality. What time are you planning to go to the hotel and where is the bomb I asked you to bring?"

Before Holmes could answer there was the shrill shriek of police whistles and a loud voice yelled, "No one move."

Suddenly there were at least a dozen constables in the pub and each of us was pulled from his chair and pushed against the wall. "What's the meaning of this?" Michael bellowed.

"You shut yer mouth, boyo, or I'll shut it fer ya," a burly constable yelled.

We were all searched for weapons and a few pistols and knives were confiscated. Then we were handcuffed and paraded outside where a police wagon was waiting for us at the kerb. Just before we climbed up, Holmes turned to me and while pretending to rub his eye, held a finger up to his lips indicating that I should remain silent.

After we had all been loaded in, the horses set off at a brisk canter. I soon realized we were headed for the Bow Street Police Station which had opened just a few years previously. There we were split into two smaller groups and placed in separate cells. As luck would have it, Holmes and I became separated. He wound up with Michael and two other lads in one cell while Jimmy and I and a third man – Liam, I believe his name was – were locked up next to them.

Over the course of the next few hours, they took us out one by one and questioned us about the robberies that had been taking place. Jimmy was taken first, and when he returned, we couldn't speak because I was summoned next. At the same time, I saw one of the men from the other cell being brought to a different room.

I was ushered into a small office that contained a table and two chairs. Sitting in the chair facing the door was a police inspector whom I had never seen before. He gestured for me to sit in the other chair while the constable stood by the door.

"Your name is Hamish Watson?"

"'Tis," I replied.

"And you work on the docks."

"I do."

When I said nothing further, he continued, "What do you know about the spate of thefts that occurred on Oxford Street and St. James Street recently?"

"Nothin' 'cept that they occurred."

"Think carefully," he advised. "Perhaps you may recall hearing something about them from a co-worker or one of the pub patrons."

I shook my head. "And even if I did – I'm no snitch."

"That's the problem with you Irish," he said. "You're all as thick as thieves. Perhaps a week or two in gaol will loosen your tongue."

"Are you arresting me?" I asked. "If so, I should like to know the charges levied against me – I believe that is my right as an Englishman."

Looking at the constable, he said, "In case you haven't noticed they're all barristers when they're not busy robbing shops and bombing railway stations."

Looking at me, he asked, "If you are English, because you certainly sound it, what are you doing with the likes of those blackguards?"

I hesitated, uncertain what my next move was to be, when he asked the constable. "Anything in his pockets?"

"Two pounds and some coins."

"Get him out of here and bring in the next one." As we were leaving, the inspector said to the constable, "Extend to him the hospitality of our lodgings for this evening, courtesy of the Crown." Then he looked at me and said, "If I were you, I'd be keeping to the straight and narrow and know that I'm going to be keeping an eye on you."

When I was returned to our cell, Liam was taken out, giving Jimmy and me the opportunity to compare notes. Our experiences with the inspector had been almost identical, and when Liam returned, his story matched ours.

In the morning, we were roused from sleep by a constable bellowing, "Time to go, gents." As he opened the cell, door, Liam walked out and I followed. As Jimmy moved to join us, the constable said, "Not so fast, mate. The inspector would like a few more words with you."

Looking back, I saw Jimmy plunge his hands into his coat pockets – the left one of which was partially ripped and had been badly repaired. As we passed the next cell, I looked in and saw none of the men, including Holmes, had yet been released. Liam and I then headed for the Ten Bells to wait for our comrades. About an hour later, after we had finished eating breakfast, Michael and the other two men entered.

Michael looked around and said, "Do they still have Jimmy?"

Liam spoke, saying, "The copper told us the inspector wanted a few more words with 'im."

"That's just grand," Michael exclaimed, and then he added, "They said the same t'ing about Fergus."

"What do you wanna do?" asked Liam.

"We'll give them an hour and then we'll hafta make other plans."

We sat there in silence with the time hanging heavy upon us. Finally, Michael looked at his watch and said, "I can't delay any more. I have business I must take care of. Let's plan to meet back here tonight at seven."

I walked home in a state of bewilderment. A thousand questions were whirling about in my brain? "Why had the police seized us? Where was Holmes? Had they connected Jimmy's ripped coat to the thefts, and if they had what did it mean?"

I entered the flat and was stunned to have a hand clapped over my mouth from behind. A voice hissed in my ear, "Watson, don't make a sound."

I nodded that I understood. I turned about to see Holmes smiling broadly, "I see a night in a cell at Bow Street has done neither of us any harm."

"Holmes, how? Why?"

"Come, Watson, surely even you can see the why?"

"No, I'm afraid I can't."

"I needed us all to be taken into custody to thwart Michael's plan to blow up the men from the Orange Order. They had their meeting early this morning and are already on their way to Liverpool whence they will catch a boat to Ireland."

"Rather a drastic measure, wouldn't you say?"

"Not at all, as it serves several other purposes as well."

"Care to enlighten me?"

"Not just yet, old friend. Your face is an open book as we know all too well. Has Michael given you any orders?"

"We are to meet back at the pub tonight at seven?"

"When you go, bring this," instructed Holmes, holding up a small bag.

"What is it?"

"It's a small bomb. You're in no danger; I've seen to that. Give it to Michael and tell him you picked it up in the alley behind the Langham Hotel where I had left it for his man."

"Won't you be there?"

"No, my friend. I have more pressing matters to which I must attend."

"I don't understand."

"I know I am asking a great deal, old man, but now more than ever I need your trust. Also, should Michael ask, and I am certain he will, all of the bombs are currently hidden, and for a small fee, you'll be happy to retrieve them for him."

"Holmes, I'm not certain I can make him believe me. You are the actor. I'm merely stage dressing."

"No, Watson, you are far more than that. You are an understudy and tonight is your night to take center stage."

Holmes then told me where he had hidden the bombs and how to make my story believable when I was confronted by Michael. He also promised he would return as soon as possible.

Holmes then changed into his constable's disguise and headed out into the bright afternoon sun. I really had no idea what game he was playing, but I had been given my orders, and by God, I would carry them out.

I spent the rest of the day trying to sleep and not really succeeding. Finally, around six, I dressed and went to Ten Bells, figuring I would eat before the meeting with Michael. A tasty shepherd's pie and a tankard of ale went some ways towards reviving my spirits.

Just before the hour, Michael walked in accompanied by Liam and Jimmy. I looked at Jimmy and said, "I'm glad you're free, but where's Fergus?"

"I dunno," he replied. "After you got out, they started releasing the fellas in the other cell. They held onto Fergus the same as me. Only he went first fer the extra questions. He musta really riled the inspector for when he came back, he had a bloody lip and a mouse under his right eye. They threw him back in the cell and then they come fer me.

"The inspector kept badgerin' me about the robberies in the posh neighborhoods, but I just kept insistin' I knew nothin' about it. Finally, I said, 'Either charge me wif somethin' or set me free. He had no proof of anythin' so here am I."

Before I could ask the question, Michael said, "Did Fergus say anythin' to you about the bombs?"

"He said if he wasn't here by ten, Hamish would tell us where the bombs are."

At that, Michael turned to me, "Well Hamish, do ya know where the bombs be?"

"I know where one is for certain," I said, holding up the Gladstone bag. "Fergus told me he left it behind the hotel as he was preparin', so I went and got it today before anyone else found it."

"What about the rest of the bombs? Do yer know where they are?"

Summoning up my courage, I said, "I suppose I could be persuaded to take you to them for a price."

At that, Michael smiled, "Just like yer partner, ain't cha?" Then he pulled back his coat to reveal a pistol in the waistband of trousers, lowered his voice and growled, "We'll wait 'til ten to see if Fergus shows up, if he don't and you don't take me to them bombs, you'll be reunited with your saintly mum far sooner than either of you expected. I trust I make myself clear."

It was the first time I had ever seen Michael make such an open threat. I don't know why but the image of him struggling to load a barrel on a wagon flashed across my mind, and I knew that he was not making an idle boast.

I nodded, and then it was if he not threatened me just seconds before. It was all smiles and laughter as they ordered another round and began chatting amongst themselves. I thought about making a break for it, but then I noticed one of Michael's men standing by the door. Even if I were to get away, I really had no idea where to go. I sat there sipping my pint and wondering how I could possibly extricate myself from this situation.

I must have been deep in thought, for suddenly I felt a hand on my shoulder, and I heard Jimmy ask, "Didn' ya hear, Michael?"

I shook off my reverie, in time to hear Michael say, "Don't make me repeat meself a third time. It's ten o'clock, Hamish, and let me just add, it's in yer best interest not to lead us on a wild goose chase, if you take my meaning'."

Chapter 15

Michael, Jimmy and I set out on foot for the Liverpool Street Station which had been constructed a decade before as the terminus for the Great Eastern Railway. After we had been walking for about five minutes, I spotted a growler. "You might want to hail that cab. The bombs are in a trunk, and I don't t'ink you want to be haulin' such a chest through the streets of London."

He agreed and five minutes later, the carriage deposited us at the entrance to the station. Michael asked the driver to wait then he turned to me and said, "Lead the way, Hamish."

I went to the left-luggage area and informed the clerk I was there to pick up a trunk and a small bag that had been sent ahead for George Berry. While the clerk went to fetch them, Michael turned to me and said, "Your friend, Fergus, has a most unusual sense of humour."

"I don't take yer meanin'," I admitted.

"And you call yourself an Irishman," he scoffed. "George Berry was the name Ricard O'Sullivan Burke gave to the police when he was arrested back in the '60s. Now don't be tellin' me, ya don't know who O'Sullivan Burke is."

Fortunately, all the research I had done on the history of the movement now stood me in good stead. I then related what I had learned about Burke. How he had left Ireland, fought in the American Civil War, and then returned to England where he had helped secure guns and blasting caps for the Brotherhood. Arrested in 1867, Burke was remanded to Clerkenwell where the Brotherhood used explosives in an attempt to free him. "If I remember the second blast destroyed sixty feet of the prison wall and killed twelve people."

"Casualties of war," said Michael indifferently.

"I believe Burke returned to America after he was released."

"Ya do know your history fer the most part," Michael said. "I'll give ya that."

"I learned a lot at my father's knee," I replied.

Just then the clerk returned dragging a trunk behind him with a small Gladstone perched atop. He dropped the handle by which he was dragging it and the front half of the trunk hit the floor with a loud thud. I know I winced and perhaps Michael and Jimmy reacted in some way as well because the clerk asked, "Something wrong?"

"I'm picking these up for my employer," I replied. "He said there would be some glassware in the trunk."

"Oh, I am sorry, sir," the clerk replied, "but I didn't hear anything break so I think it's fine. Now if you will just sign here." And with that he pushed a paper towards me as he handed me a pen. After I had signed, he asked, "Do you need help with those?"

"We've got it," said Michael. He and Jimmy then each took a handle and they carried the trunk out to the growler as I followed behind with the Gladstone. We all climbed inside and set the trunk on the floor between us. When we arrived back at the Ten Bells, Jimmy ordered the barman to close the place.

We carried the trunk into the back room. Michael then took the bag from me and opened it. Inside were the blasting caps as well as various lengths of fuse. The blasting caps had each been wrapped in cloth. Next Michael tried to open the trunk at which point, he discovered it was locked. "Do you have the key?"

Deciding that discretion would be the better part of valour, I was considering trying to escape and get to the police so that I could tell them about Michael possessing the bombs. Although I trusted Holmes, it just seemed as if there were too many things that could go wrong with this plan. Still, if I failed to get to the police, this could all end in tragedy, so I decided to stay the course.

Although lying has never come easy to me, at that point, I could think of nothing else so I said, "Fergus has one key, but there is another back in the flat. I'll fetch it for you." So saying, I rose and headed for the door.

All of sudden Michael said, "Hold a bit there, Hamish." He then had a brief conversation with Jimmy before he announced, "Jimmy will go wif you just to make certain nothin' happens to you. Whitechapel can be a very dangerous place at night."

We walked to the flat, passing the usual denizens of the evening on the streets, and despite my protestations, Jimmy followed me inside. I went to the mantel and pretended to search there. "He must've moved it," I said. "It's not here."

"Well then we'd better search the flat until we find it. It wouldn't be in anyone's best interest to return without it."

Jimmy began looking through the cupboards, examining each dish and bowl. I puttered about the fireplace. After about ten minutes, I heard Jimmy mutter, "It's just not here." Glancing in my direction, he said, "Who plays cricket?"

Feigning surprise, I exclaimed, "That's it!" And I ran to the cricket bat leaning in the corner. After I had picked it up, I found the key right where Holmes had said it would be – affixed to the bottom with a piece of surgical tape that had been colored to blend in with the wood.

"I should've thought of this sooner."

"Well, I'm glad you did. That's a very clever hidin' place."

"Would you expect anything else from someone like Fergus?"

Key in hand, we headed back to the Ten Bells where Michael was waiting for us. "What took you so long?"

"Fergus hid the key in a new spot, but Hamish found it," Jimmy informed him.

"Good work," exclaimed Michael. "Now give it 'ere."

He then opened the trunk. Inside were all thirty bombs, each of which consisted of three or five sticks of dynamite. All of the bombs had been carefully wrapped in a thick towel so that there was little room for slippage in the trunk.

"Well, it would seem we have everything we need – except Mr. Fergus and his timing devices." Glancing at me, Michael asked, "I don't suppose you know anything about placin' bombs, do you Mr. Hamish."

I laughed, "You don't want me playin' around with those things, and truth be told, I've no desire to be anywhere near them. Even standin' this close makes me a bit uneasy. Maybe you won't need timers for all of them. I know that Fergus makes those fuses special so that they burn very slowly. He coats 'em with some kind of chemical mixture so they do that."

"Well that is a bit of good news. You wouldn't know exactly how slow they burn, I suppose, or the chemicals he treats them with?"

"I'm afraid I can't help you there. He's very secretive about his methods – as you've probably noticed."

"There's certainly no disputin' that," said Jimmy.

"I admire your honesty, Hamish, but at the same time your lack of skill still leaves me wantin'. I suppose we'll just have to test a fuse and see what we learn," said Michael.

"Do you still plan to start bombing," at the point the bells in the nearby Christ Church rang for midnight, "tomorrow?"

"No need to worry about my plans, Hamish. The less you know, the less you can tell the police if yer arrested again. Now let's meet back here tonight at eight, and then we can talk about who's doin' what tomorrow."

As I left, I looked back to see Michael withdrawing the bombs from the trunk and placing them on the table in front of him.

As I walked home, I wondered if, given Holmes' absence, Michael might turn to the mysterious Daire. I thought perhaps Michael might bring him to the meeting when he gave each of us our assignments. It suddenly hit me then, how similar Holmes and Michael were. Both were meticulous planners who played things close to the vest, and both obviously had prepared other options in case the first plan should fail.

Although he was angry at the spanner thrown into the works by Fergus' absence, he obviously had Daire in reserve for just such an emergency. I couldn't wait to relay my deductions, such as they were, to Holmes. And then I was struck by the thought that if I had been able to figure it out, Holmes must have arrived at the same conclusion days ago.

I checked the front door as I entered the building, but there were no chalk marks. I was half hoping to find Holmes sitting before the fire and the flat filled with the malodorous fumes of his shag tobacco. However, when I opened the door, the flat was empty and my hopes were dashed. With few options left to me, I turned in but sleep did not come easily as I tossed and turned most of the night.

I awoke the next morning with a feeling of dread in my stomach. I had not heard from Holmes for more than a day and the bombing campaign was supposed to begin the next day. I thought about going to see Lestrade, but as the inspector was unpredictable; there was always the chance that he might just swoop in and arrest all the Fenians – a move that could undo all of Holmes' careful planning. At times like this I was angry for my friend's lack of trust in me.

Uncertain what to do next, I decided to remain in the flat on the chance that Holmes would return. When I stepped out for lunch, I asked Julie to keep an eye out for Fergus. Upon my return, she said, she had seen no one.

The afternoon and early evening dragged by, and I left for the Ten Bells about half seven, still wondering where Holmes might be. When I entered the pub, I saw Michael, Jimmy, Liam and two other men at a table in the rear. I wondered if one of the newcomers might be the mysterious Daire.

As I took a seat at the table, Michael asked, "Still no sign of Fergus?"

"No, he must still be in police custody." I then turned to the two new men and introduced myself. One told me his name was Stephen and the other said he was called Brian.

Michael interrupted me by saying, "Let's get to business, shall we? Tomorrow at noon there is a special mass at Westminster Abbey. I'd originally thought to offer a personal greeting to the

Archbishop of Canterbury wishing him a happy May Day, but I don't want our boys travelin' that far. So we'll have to content ourselves with the Anglicans at Westminster." At that, everyone chuckled, and my mind began to race, thinking how I might avoid this tragedy.

Michael continued, "I was considering two surprises for our friends tomorrow, and that may still happen. With Fergus in jail, we have but one experienced bomber. Although the fuses that Mr. Fergus provided will give anyone who's willing a four or five-minute head start." Again everybody at the table laughed.

"Now, here's what I want everyone to do. Jimmy, your job is go to Bow Street and see what if anyt'ing can be done to free Mr. Fergus. Every few hours try to git in to see him."

"I'll do me best," replied Jimmy.

"Stephen and Brian – you're on guard duty tonight. You know where to go?"

They both nodded their assent.

"All right then, I'll be seeing you bright and early at seven."

"What about me?" I asked. "What is my assignment?"

"Ah, Hamish, I have something very special in mind for you. Meet me at half six at the corner of Folgate Street and Commercial Street. Since yer the only one among us with even the slightest experience with dynamite, I want you with me tomorrow. Oh, and wear yer best outfit. We might be going someplace a bit posh."

I was stunned and confused. On the one hand, it seemed as though I might be able to prevent whatever Michael had planned. However, I realized that I knew next to nothing about explosives and was fearful of being found out. Opting to see the glass half full, I decided any course of action would be better than doing nothing.

The next morning I rose at six. I dressed in my best clothing which was still quite shabby by normal standards, and set out to meet Michael. Just as I reached the front door, our neighbor, Julie, entered the building. I wondered what might have got her up so early, but I had little time for pleasantries. I told her that if she saw Fergus, he should meet me as soon as possible at the intersection of Folgate and Commercial.

As I walked along Commercial, I saw Michael in the distance, leaning against a lamp post. When I got closer he exclaimed, "*Abair latha math da na h-Eirennaich!*" When I looked at him in confusion, he replied, "I fergot, yer dinna speak Irish. I was just saying, 'What a great day fer the Irish.' He then continued, "I dinna t'ink it will be such a great day for the English." And then he laughed.

My blood was boiling but I fought to bring my emotions under control. "So what's the plan?" I asked with all the nonchalance I could muster.

"Since, according to Jimmy, Fergus is still in gaol, Daire will carry out the second of today's bombings, and we will carry out the first."

I must admit, I was taken aback to discover that Michael had actually planned two bombings. However, since our bomb was to be set off first, there was a chance I might be able to foil his plan. Unfortunately, I had no idea what time or where exactly in Westminster Abbey, the other explosion might take place.

"Before we do anything," he said breaking into my thoughts, "I think we should get some breakfast. Don't know about you, but

I'm starvin' – although I'm nowhere near as hungry as I have been in the past."

We went out of our way to go to the White Swan on Alle Street. "Won't we be late?" I objected.

"No, we've plenty of time. Where we're goin', it doesn't open 'til nine o'clock, and it's not even two miles away."

I had clues, and now I had to think like Holmes. I thought about how Trinity Square Gardens and the London Wall were close enough. As we walked I wracked my brains and realized the Tower of London was not that far either. And then I realized wherever we were headed, it would have to be a last-minute attempt on my part to avert disaster, and then I would have to hope for the best at Westminster – if I could get there in time.

Michael ordered a breakfast of bacon and sausage with two fried eggs. I ordered toast with jam that I cannot recall tasting, so preoccupied was I with thoughts of thwarting Michael's plan. After finishing, we left the pub and headed for Turner Street. As we approached the house with the basement in the rear, I saw Brian standing guard in the front. We went around to the back where Stephen was sitting outside the basement, smoking a cigarette.

"Far better you smoke out here than in there," said Michael pointing to the cellar.

"What? You think I'm an eejit?" asked Stephen.

Michael laughed, "I know you're a bright lad, but some of your friends ..." and he let his words trail off. We then entered the cellar, and I saw the trunk sitting to one side. The lid was up and there were still a number of towels visible, but without pulling each one out, I couldn't determine the exact number of bombs that remained. As Michael moved to the table, I noticed a pair of unusual looking cases on it.

"What are they?" I inquired.

"I'd like to say they're an invention of me own, but Daire came up with the idea," he said proudly throwing open the lid of one. "It's actually a case for a sackbut, but it suits our needs just fine."

"I don't understand."

"Look," he said holding up the case so that I could examine the inside. "Daire has wound the fuse the length and breadth of the case – top and bottom. Since the fuse burns at the rate of a foot every thirty seconds, we have between four and five minutes to make our escape after it's lit."

I saw the fuse running just as Michael had described with the bomb nestled safely at one end – wedged in so it could not move. I remember thinking, "That is fiendishly clever."

Michael then closed the case and called to Stephen, "Are you done smoking? If not, don't come in here."

"I'm done," he said as he descended the stairs. Picking up the sackbut case, he handed it to Stephen and said, "You know what to do?"

"Aye."

"Take Brian with you and good luck to the both of yer. Remember – five minutes at the most!"

He saluted Michael and said, "You can count on us."

I looked at Michael, who was now examining the second case, "Won't someone be suspicious of your carrying a sackbut case into wherever we are going?"

He laughed, "Under ordinary circumstances they might, but I've arranged for a special concert of music to be performed. We'll just be members of the band."

"I have no instrument."

Reaching behind him into the trunk, he pulled out a flute case. "Now you're a flautist. There's even a real flute in there in case you get stopped. I don't suppose you'd care to entertain us."

I was desperately seeking a way to extricate myself from this predicament, when it hit me. "Surely you don' t'ink I'll be doin' this for free."

"If all goes well, you'll receive Fergus's £50 and maybe a wee bit extra as a bonus. Now let's get going. We have time, but I certainly don't want us to be late."

"Where exactly are we goin?"

"It's a surprise, Hamish. Everyone likes surprises."

We walked down to Commercial Road and then almost to Back Church Lane before we were able to hail a cab. Michael told the driver our destination, but I was unable to hear what he said.

My stomach was in knots as we turned onto Hooper Street and then Dock Street and headed towards the waterfront. I took hope. If we were targeting a ship, perhaps I could rally the crew and some dockworkers and stop Michael with their assistance. However, we soon left the docks behind when we turned onto East Smithfield and then onto Tower Road. A short while later, we stopped with the Trinity Square Gardens on our right and the Tower of London on our left.

I alighted from the cab and started walking towards the gardens, but Michael soon corrected me, "Yer goin' the wrong way." I then followed him towards the Tower. As it was now nearing half nine, there were a number of sightseers queued up and waiting to enter. I also spotted several carrying musical instrument cases among the crowd. So far Michael's plan was falling together nicely. We entered and quickly walked past St. Thomas's Tower, the Wakefield Tower and the Lanthorn Tower. We entered the courtyard at the Bloody Tower and then Michael made for the White Tower.

"Where are we going?" I asked, actually breathing a sigh of relief as there were no people near us.

"We're here, laddy."

Suddenly I heard the raucous caw of a bird, and my heart sank in my chest, for I realized Michael had come to test the legend.

Chapter 16

"You know the old story? There must forever be ravens at the Tower, and if they should leave, the Tower will crumble to dust, the Crown will fall and England with it."

I could only nod, having first heard the tale when I was a boy. I knew it dated back to King Charles II, and most subjects had come to put some degree of faith, however small, in it as the Crown made it a point to keep captive ravens at the Tower.

"I dinna believe it myself, but I ken hope 'tis true."

"What are you saying?"

"Sometimes destroying a symbol can have a greater effect than winnin' a battle." With that he walked towards the ravens' cages. I kept looking for a Yeoman Warder, but could find none.

Michael then placed his case right in front of the cages, bent down, pulled out a lucifer and lit the fuse, the end of which was just visible through a small hole that had been drilled in the case. "I think it's best, we leave this place behind us."

At that moment, a group of perhaps ten or twelve children, accompanied by two nuns turned the far corner from the Bloody Tower. It was obvious that they were coming to see the birds and then I noticed a Maypole had been erected on the lawn.

I looked at Michael, and said, "They're but children."

To which he replied, "War demands sacrifices."

"Innocent youngsters and nuns – that image will hurt your cause more than help it. You must see that."

"Well, there's nothing I can do. The fuse has been lit." With that he turned and started running back the way we had come.

"You coward," I seethed. Not knowing exactly what I was going to do, I ran to the case, picked it up and flung it as far as I could toward the battlements in front of the Traitors' Gate. It hit the ground just as I threw myself on the youngsters in front and told the others to get down. We remained there prostrate and when I managed a furtive glance, I saw Michael still sprinting for all he was worth back towards the entrance to the Tower.

Suddenly, I heard a voice say, "Bravo, Watson. I really must commend you."

Looking up, I saw a bearded, bespectacled gentleman, perhaps a banker or solicitor standing some ten or twelve feet away. Although he looked nothing like Holmes, the voice I had heard was most definitely my friend's. In an instant, I realized it was indeed Holmes.

Jumping up, I yelled, "Holmes, Michael's getting away."

"He won't get far. Trust me."

"There's a second bomb, Holmes. It's going to go off in …"

Before I could finish my sentence, he said, "The Crystal Palace. Not to worry, we have that under control as well. By the bye, how was your breakfast? You certainly didn't eat …"

"…Westminster Abbey."

"What?" Holmes stopped talking and looked at me incredulously, "Are you absolutely certain?"

"I believe so. I know nothing about a bomb at the Crystal Palace, but Michael told me this morning about the blast planned for Westminster. He even said that Daire was going to place it.

He entrusted a case similar to this to a young man named Stephen, and I assumed he was bringing it to Daire."

"The young man was carrying the bomb to the Crystal Palace. I thought he might be Daire or at least meeting Daire en route. At any rate, the police have him under surveillance and will arrest him before he is able to do any kind of mischief."

At that he lapsed into silence for a moment. When he finally spoke, his tone was one of self-recrimination. "Oh, Watson, I have underestimated Michael badly. When he told us how he liked to keep things separated, I totally grasped his concept, and I have been anticipating two bombings ever since that time. I must admit I never expected three.

"Come, we must get to Westminster with all due haste." As we headed for the Traitors' Gate, Holmes picked up the sackbut case. "You never know, this may come in handy."

"We were very lucky that didn't go off."

Holmes pooh-poohed me, "Once again, luck had nothing to do with it. In every fuse but one, I inserted a six-inch section of asbestos fibers. That's why I covered the fuses with a thick coat of lacquer. I had you tell Michael it was to make them burn more slowly, but actually it was to make certain they were never carefully inspected and thus halt the detonation process."

"You said there was one fuse you didn't treat? How could you be certain that Michael didn't burn a bad fuse and tumble to your plan?"

"Michael has been under surveillance constantly for the past month – either by Wiggins, myself, Smith or one of his men from the Special Irish Branch. By the way, Smith is not nearly so set against disguises as you are."

"The fuses?"

"I saw Michael purchase two sackbut cases over the course of two days about a week and a half ago – just the cases, mind, no instruments."

"I knew immediately what he had in mind. As a result, all the fuses I gave him were ten feet long; however, there was one that was only five feet long – I knew it wouldn't serve his purpose with the sackbut cases, and I banked on him using that as his test fuse."

"You took an incredible gamble, Holmes."

"I prefer to regard it as a carefully weighed risk, but as I've said before … desperate times. Besides, I had factored everything into my calculations."

"Except the third bomb."

Holmes winced and said, "If Daire has used one of my fuses, we are home free, However, if he likes to do everything himself … Well, I'd rather not think of that at the moment."

By this time, we had left the Tower behind, and Holmes sprinted towards the Thames – sackbut case in hand. I was doing my best to keep up, but he had the better of me. I saw him scanning the Thames and obviously there were no passenger vessels in sight. "Blast! A boat would have been much faster. Let us hail a cab and hope for the best."

We then ran past the Byward Tower and out through the Middle Tower. Despite my aching leg, I was keeping relatively close to Holmes, who was slowed a bit by the weight of the case. We ran past some stunned visitors and out to Three Quays Walk where we finally hailed a cab on Lower Thames Street.

"Westminster Abbey," yelled Holmes, "and there's an extra sovereign in it if you don't spare the horses."

"I'll do me best, guv, but they's been workin' all night."

The driver cracked his whip, and we set off at a brisk trot. As you might imagine, Holmes was the picture of impatience. After a minute, the driver yelled down, "London Bridge or Upper Thames Street."

"Whichever's faster," Holmes replied.

"I'll stick to the land then and hope for the best," he said.

Although I didn't want to disturb my friend, I felt as though I had to ask the question: "Holmes, how will you spot Daire?"

"I'm working on that as we speak, Watson. Now, exercise that rare gift of silence which I know you possess; hopefully, I can find a way to atone for my past shortcomings in this case."

We passed Waterloo Bridge and turned onto the Embankment. The driver was making excellent time, and Holmes was continuing his silence. As we turned on Bridge Street, I saw Holmes perk up. I had no idea what had roused him from his lethargy. "At the Tower of London, I told you that I had badly underestimated Michael. Do you recall?"

"Indeed, it wasn't but fifteen or twenty minutes ago."

"If I am right, I think Michael may have underestimated me as well."

"By me – do you mean yourself or Fergus?"

"A touch, Watson. I think Michael may have overestimated his cleverness, but I must say there is no denying the man's Machiavellian nature."

"Holmes, keeping up with this conversation is proving more difficult than keeping pace with you at the Tower."

"I am sorry, old friend. My mind makes these leaps." He then explained to me the conclusions he had arrived at regarding Michael and the third bomber. When he had finished, I could only stare at him in disbelief. "Holmes, that is monstrous! What's to be done?"

"Everything in our powers, old friend. That is all we can do."

By this time, we had turned onto the Broad Sanctuary, and Holmes then explained exactly what he had planned. As we pulled up in front of the Abbey, Holmes jumped from the cab. "It is now just half-ten. I believe we have perhaps an hour and a half, two and a half at the most, to locate Daire and scotch this plan once and for all."

"I'm still not certain I follow."

"It is not widely known but somehow Michael must have learned of the fact that Prince Arthur is scheduled to attend this ceremony. If Royal protocol holds, he will arrive here between a quarter to the hour and five of twelve. I have no doubt he will be accompanied by his wife, Princess Louise Margaret. If anything were to happen to her on English soil, I'm not certain any amount of explaining would satisfy the Prussian court. At best, relations between the countries would be badly strained; at worst, well, I prefer not to dwell upon that possibility."

"Why do you say we have until one o'clock to sort this out?"

"The special service is in honor of Prince Albert, who is visiting his mother. You may recall the Prince is also the Duke of Connaught, one of the five ancient kingdoms or provinces of Ireland. After the ceremony, the bells of the Abbey will ring in joyous celebration, and at that time I am certain Daire will explode his bomb. My instinct tells me the bomb will target the Prince and his wife; obviously, I cannot be certain, but the logic certainly leans that way."

"How will we spot Daire?"

"He will be carrying a case of some sort in which to transport the bomb. He will do everything possible to appear inconspicuous, and I am afraid that may well work in his favour since we have no idea what he looks like."

"Holmes, we cannot possibly hope to see everyone who enters the Abbey. We need more men."

"You are right, old man. Now, here is what I want you to do."

Minutes later I found myself in a different cab speeding towards Whitechapel. Holmes had assigned the Irregulars to keep an eye on several members of the Brotherhood as well as the woman Michael had been seeing. I had to pay the driver extra to take me to Blossom Street. Even in daytime some drivers were still loath to enter Whitechapel. I held the cab and when I dismounted, I discovered two of the Irregulars – Simon, and a lad known as Crusty – lounging at the corner of Folgate and Blossom. "Boys, Mr. Holmes has need of you. Where are the others?"

"He told us to stay 'ere and to follow the lady if'n she came out."

"Has she come out?"

They shook their heads. "Well then, I'll take over your sentry duty. Do you know where any of the other Irregulars are?"

This time they nodded, and Simon said, "Daniel is across the street from the Ten Bells, John and Frank are on Varden Street and Wiggins is at Turner Street."

"Here are your new orders: Take that cab, round up as many of the boys as you can and then head to Westminster Abbey. Mr. Holmes is there and he has a very important assignment for you."

I went to the cab and installed the lads. I then gave the driver the directions and handed him a sovereign. "There's another waiting for you when you deposit the boys in front of Westminster Abbey. Now, off with you."

After a few minutes, I decided I was wasting my time and could be of far more use to Holmes at the Abbey. I decided to make certain the woman was home and then try to find a cab – no easy task in this section of the city.

I walked across the street, desperately trying to recall the landlady's name. It came to me – Francesca Gerette – just as I knocked on the door. When a petite, dark-haired woman answered, I introduced myself and asked if I might speak with her tenant, Miss O'Shea.

"She's not here," the woman replied. "She went out earlier this morning."

I tried to contain my surprise as I didn't want to frighten the woman. "Oh," I replied casually, "I was supposed to meet her here this morning."

"Ah, that Pegeen," she laughed. "She's always forgetting something."

She then invited me in for tea. I looked at my watch and decided I could give her five minutes and no more. As we chatted, she said to me, "I'm glad she listened to me. She and that Michael – always fighting and yelling."

"Oh, what were they fighting about?"

"I really couldn't say, but I am glad he's been replaced," and she chuckled again.

It struck me then that Mrs. Garette thought I was Pegeen's new beau. I also wondered how she had managed to slip past the Irregulars. I casually asked, "Does your house have a back door?"

She looked at me as if I were insane. "Of course," she replied. "It leads to a narrow alley you can use to get to Elder Street."

I had to smile at the irony of one of Holmes' most trusted tricks being used against him.

"What was she wearing?" I asked, "Perhaps I'll go look for her. I know her favourite stores."

"She had a bright green dress on. When I complimented her, she told me 'it seemed appropriate for the day.' Truth be told, I'm not quite certain what she meant by that."

"Was she carrying a bag of any kind?"

"Yes," she had a very stylish basket bag which she said she a friend wanted to borrow."

I thanked Mrs. Garette profusely and hurried out the door. "Well that's another piece removed from the board," I thought. Unfortunately, we were still no closer to finding the mysterious Daire. I had thought about asking to search Pegeen's room, but I hadn't wanted to arouse the Mrs. Garette's suspicions.

After crossing several streets. I finally was able to hail a cab, and I arrived back at Westminster at exactly half-eleven, the bells sounding the half hour as I descended from the cab.

I quickly spotted Holmes who was standing on the walkway in front of the main entrance – perhaps twenty feet from the doors. He was carefully scanning all the early arrivals. As I approached, he said, "I'm glad you're back, old man. Time is running out."

"What about the North Door?"

"I have stationed Wiggins there with three of the Irregulars. They have been instructed to find me if they should see anyone carrying a case for any kind of musical instrument or anything else they deem suspicious."

"The Abbey will be crowded, especially with Prince Arthur due to attend the service."

"Yes, that is why I feel we need to locate Daire before Prince Arthur's arrival. I would estimate that gives us about twenty-five minutes at the most. I'd like you to remain in this spot just in case the Irregulars see something."

"Certainly, and while I am standing here, what will you be doing."

"I'll be in the crowd, looking for anything that seems even slightly out of place."

"How will I summon you if I need you?"

With that Holmes handed me a police whistle. "Use it if you see anything that strikes you as out of the ordinary. Wiggins also has a whistle, so if you should hear it, head for the North Door. I will meet you there."

I watched as Holmes waded into the crowd. Because of his height, I was able to keep an eye on him for some minutes before I lost him. There were people constantly making their way towards and then into the Abbey. I was looking at faces and then I realized I had never set eyes on the man. As a result, I began to look at shoes and bags, trying to see anything that appeared the least bit out of place. I was surprised at the number of religious – both male and female – attending the service. I was also taken aback at the number of young people in the area. I supposed many of them were hoping to get a glimpse of the Prince and his wife. After several minutes, I heard the clatter of horse hooves and moved to the side as a group of six smartly dressed soldiers cleared the way for a glistening Clarence with a driver and a footman sitting atop and a coat of arms on the door. As it passed, a man, presumably Prince Arthur was waving to those in attendance, while a woman waved to the crowd on the other side.

I glanced at my watch and was surprised to see that it was five of the hour. I searched among the crowd, hoping to spot Holmes but he was out of my sight.

I watched the carriage stop in front of the doorway and saw the footman jump down. He opened the door and Prince Arthur alighted; he then turned and offered his hand to his wife. After she had stepped down, they turned and entered the church. I had heard no sound of a whistle from the Irregulars, and I had lost sight of Holmes altogether.

I looked at my watch and it was one minute before the hour. I didn't know how much time we had left; in fact, I couldn't even hazard a guess. The only thing I knew for certain is what few minutes did remain were rapidly running out.

Chapter 17

Uncertain whether to enter the church and aid in the search or remain on guard outside, I opted for the latter. I considered speaking to the footman who had accompanied the Prince's carriage and possibly ascertaining the day's itinerary. Ultimately, I decided that might arouse even more suspicion, which would be directed squarely at me, should anything untoward happen.

With the driver on duty, I decided instead to stroll over to the North Door and check on the Irregulars. When I got there, I spotted Wiggins and the other lads, waiting outside the entrance.

"Nothing to report, lads?"

"Nah," replied Wiggins. "Seems like a wild goose chase if you ask me, but Mr. 'Olmes is never wrong, so we'll stay 'ere until 'e dismisses us."

"Plus the pay's good," piped up one of the lads, causing Wiggins to shoot him a reproving look.

"Well, stay alert! Something could happen at any minute," I cautioned them as I started back towards the main entrance. As I rounded the corner, I heard footsteps behind me and turned to see Holmes running towards me.

Although he held up his finger to indicate that I should remain silent, I just had to tell him, "The woman from Turner Street slipped away from the Irregulars, but according to her landlady she's visiting a friend."

Holmes just looked at me incredulously and then he whispered, "I have been obtuse in the extreme, but I believe I am seeing clearly now."

As we reached the corner, we stopped and peered around it. A lone figure, a nun by her appearance, was walking away from the coach and the Abbey. I wondered if she had arrived late and decided to simply forego the service. All of a sudden, Holmes yelled, "I'll see to the carriage. You go after her, Watson."

I started after the woman, running as best I could, but she had a considerable head start, and by the time I reached The Sanctuary and made my way to Victoria Street, she was nowhere to be seen. I hurried back towards the church, not relishing the idea of reporting my failure to Holmes. As I drew closer, I could see him talking to the liveried footman. The other soldiers were keeping the rest of the churchgoers inside the Abbey.

Finally, I saw Holmes open the door to the carriage and look inside. By now I was close enough to ask, "Do you need any help?"

"Yes, do open the door on your side very gently then step back." He then closed the door on his side and walked around the carriage so that it was between us and the footman and anyone else who might have found a way out of the Abbey.

Having done as he bade, I peered into the carriage. In the middle of the floor sat a woven basket purse. "Is that the bomb?"

"I believe it is," he remarked calmly. As he reached into the carriage, he lifted it carefully and cradled it in his arms. "She left the basket in the coach during the service. She told the driver it was a gift from the nuns of her convent for Prince Arthur and his wife and their children," said Holmes as he walked. "I had anticipated such a move, although not by a nun, which is I why I had stationed you there."

I felt my stomach drop, but Holmes continued, "Not to worry, old friend. It is fortunate you went to check on the Irregulars;

otherwise, things might have turned out quite differently." Looking at me, he added, "You might want to stay some distance back. I have no idea what type of detonator is in here nor when it will go off."

"Well," I said, "I guess we will find out together, won't we."

"Good old Watson."

By now we were passing the Abbot's Hall and then Holmes surprised me when he made a left turn and started walking down a path towards the rear of the church. "Not that I mean to pry, but where exactly are we headed?"

He didn't answer me, but he then turned right and then made another turn to the left, and suddenly we were in a covered walkway of stone with a magnificent courtyard on our left. "These are the Cloisters, old man. Now, do me a favour and clamber over that wall." I did as Holmes asked and then turned to face him.

"I am going to hand you the basket while I climb over. Try to keep it level, and do be gentle with it."

So saying, he handed me the basket, and two seconds later he was taking it back from me. Holmes continued walking, and as I turned around, I realised his intent. In the middle of the greensward was a large fountain. Holmes reached it, knelt down quite carefully and gently lowered the basket into the water; he held it under with his hand.

"How much longer must we wait?"

"I think another minute or two should do it. The baptismal font might have been closer but there was always the chance of people panicking and starting a stampede. During the crush to exit the Abbey, someone might have jarred the basket, and again there was the issue of the detonator."

"I am certain you made the right choice; moreover there is no predicting how the Prince and Princess might have reacted, let alone the crowd. I am certain the congregation might have found the sight of a man dunking a basket in the baptismal font most unsettling. Also, in the panic that sight might have engendered among the crowd, anything might have happened."

A minute later Holmes lifted the sodden basket from the fountain and gingerly opened the lid. "Clever, very clever," he murmured. "Look at this, Watson. They have secured four lucifers against a fold of abrasive paper. In opening the lid, the matches would have ignited this short fuse immediately and detonation would have occurred in no more than ten or fifteen seconds."

"The woman who left the basket appeared to be a nun," I sputtered.

"Yes, and I have appeared to be many things. Your point?"

"Was that Daire?"

"I can't imagine it was anyone else."

"But I thought Daire was a man."

"That's what Michael wanted us to think. If you recall, anytime you or I referred to Daire it was as 'he,' Michael never corrected us."

"So when and how did you come to realize that Daire was actually a woman."

"I can lay no claim to glory in this case, old friend, for I have been criminally slow and it almost cost us – and the Kingdom –

dearly. But to answer your question, I was searching the Abbey looking for Daire and only half paying attention to what the priest was saying during his sermon. Had I been listening more carefully, I might have caught her in the act. Although that might not have been the best course of action either."

"Obviously, something the priest said struck you."

"Indeed, he was talking about Ireland and the meaning of the name Patrick, the patron saint of that country. You will recall that Prince Arthur is also Duke of Connaught. At any rate, Patrick comes from the Latin word *patricius,* which means of noble birth. Hence our word patrician."

"Holmes…"

"My apologies. At that point, I started to think about what Daire meant. As you know it is an Irish name that is generally, although obviously not always, given to boys as it means 'oak tree.' However, there is a second meaning of 'fruitful' or 'fertile.' At that moment, I realized we had been on the wrong scent. I can only surmise that her father desperately wanted a son and when a daughter was born, he gave the baby a boy's name. My worst fears were confirmed when you said Miss O'Shea had left the house undetected by the Irregulars.

"As I watched the priest bless himself at the end of the homily, I suddenly recalled Michael's fondness for 'threes.' When we first met him he was wearing a shamrock pin. Every time there was a toast, he made certain to invoke three names or concepts – even if he had to add to another's toast. I should have seen three bombers long before I did.

"Now, knowing that Daire could be a male or a female, I left via the North Door and instructed Wiggins to be on the lookout for any women carrying baskets or cases. When I learned you had just been there, I sprinted hard to catch up to you whereupon you confirmed my suspicions."

"What do we do now, Holmes? We have foiled the plot – for the moment. However, there is nothing to stop them from regrouping."

"You sum it up succinctly, Watson. As the Bard might have said, 'We have scotched the snake, not killed it. She'll close and be herself while our poor malice remains in danger of her former tooth.'"

"*Macbeth*?"

"Bravo! He says those words right after he kills Banquo but Fleance escapees, so the threat to his crown continues. Now let us get in touch with Scotland Yard. I'll explain everything to Lestrade and Smith. They can forward the briefing to Mister Orr."

"And what will we be doing?"

"Come, Watson, even you can figure out what our next move must be." Having made his pronouncement, he lifted the sopping basket from the grass, turned on his heel and headed for the wall. Once over it we made our way to the street and hailed a hansom. "Scotland Yard," Holmes instructed the driver.

We were in the cab but a minute or two when Holmes bade the driver stop. He then jumped out and returned with several newspapers. I had no idea what he was looking for, and it seemed both imprudent and impudent to ask. He spent the next several minutes quickly looking through the papers, spending no more than a minute on each. With the fourth paper, he exclaimed, "Aha!" He then tore a page from the paper, folded it and placed it in his pocket.

It was but two minutes later when we arrived at the Yard. Although Lestrade was in, it appeared as though Smith were out of the office. Holmes left word with the sergeant to have Smith join us and Inspector Lestrade as soon as he returned. We then made our way to Lestrade's office with Holmes still lugging the wet basket while I had been entrusted with the sackbut case.

After we had deposited our trophies on the floor next to Lestrade's desk, Holmes then gave the inspector a rather superficial account of our recent activities, which was punctuated by questions from Lestrade such as, "So then you have been working on this case since January?"

Holmes merely nodded.

Lestrade continued, "And I suppose you and Dr. Watson never went to America at all?"

"A necessary deception I'm afraid, Inspector," said Holmes.

"The only person who knew we didn't go was Mrs. Hudson," I added. "And we didn't even want to tell her, but it was necessary."

As you might expect, Lestrade was equal parts confusion, effusive in his praise, and angry at not having been told the truth. Just then there was a knock on the door. "Enter," said Lestrade and Smith came into the room – his face the picture of joy.

Before anyone could say anything, Smith said, "We got him Mr. Holmes. He was rather easy to spot, carrying that sackbut case."

"Who? Who did you get?" roared Lestrade.

"The bloke what was going to bomb the Crystal Palace. Fortunately, Mr. Holmes told us what to look for. We nicked him at the gate and although he's not talking, he didn't give us any trouble."

"And the bomb?" inquired Holmes.

"We pulled the blasting cap out and soaked the sticks in water just to be sure."

"That won't render them totally harmless, but do keep them submerged for the time being. Otherwise, you have done well," replied my friend. "You gentlemen have accomplished yeoman work this day – foiling three bombing attempts in one morning and saving the lives of Prince Arthur and Princess Louise."

Smith began to protest, "But without your warning…"

Holmes just waved dismissively in Smith's direction. After he had attempted to renew his protest, Lestrade interrupted him.

"Don't argue with him," the inspector said, now somewhat mollified when he realized Holmes wanted his involvement in the affair to remain secret. "I've learned from our years together that Mr. Holmes would rather the official force receive the credit." Turning to Holmes, he continued, "What is it you like to say? 'The work is its own reward.'"

"Still doesn't seem cricket, but if that's the way you want it, that's most generous of you Mr. Holmes," said Smith.

"I do, but this particular case carries with it one caveat."

"Just name it, Mr. Holmes," said Lestrade, "and if it is in my power to grant it, you shall have it."

Holmes then told both inspectors what he wished. When he had finished, Lestrade looked at Smith and said, "It's certainly irregular, but I have no objections, if you don't."

"That's all you wish, Mr. Holmes?"

"That's all I want," replied my friend.

"Done," said Smith and we then shook hands all around.

"Now, if you will excuse us, Dr. Watson and I have some business to which we must attend."

Before we left the office, Holmes turned back and pulled an envelope from his jacket pocket. "Here is a list of all the associates that Watson and I have encountered during this investigation as well as the pubs they frequent. Whenever possible, I have provided addresses but I'm afraid you will find my list wanting in that regard. Still, if you move quickly …"

We then bade the inspectors good day and promised we would keep in touch.

When we were in the carriage, I said, "Holmes, a question."

"Just one?" he laughed.

"Was the list you gave Lestrade and Smith complete?"

"I may have inadvertently left off one or two names," he said with a smile. "Now, I must think."

With that he lapsed into one of his familiar poses – chin pressed to his chest, eyes half closed.

I could not say exactly what he was thinking, but in this one instance, I believed I had a pretty fair idea.

Chapter 18

After a brief stop at Baker Street, during which we both packed small bags and enjoyed a light lunch, Holmes summoned the page and told him to secure a cab for us. As we descended the stairs a moment later, Holmes turned to me and said, "I do hope that you have brought along your Army pistol."

I patted the pocket of my greatcoat to indicate that I had.

"Splendid," he replied. "Hopefully, we'll have no need of it. Still, it's always best to prepare for the worst."

We headed for Euston and arrived with a few minutes to spare before our train. I knew our journey would be a long one and since I could never tell when Holmes might lapse into one of his uncommunicative silences, I had brought a book along, a copy of Shorthouse's *John Inglesant,* which I had received as a Christmas gift from a patient.

Although it is not the type of story I might choose on my own, I was quite enjoying the intrigue. Admittedly, I could have done with a bit less debate. I was considering the hero's remarks on Quietism when Holmes suddenly broke the silence. "I've been thinking, Watson, and truth be told, I find myself in something of a quandry."

"With regard to what?"

"I'm not certain what to do with Michael when we capture him."

"Surely, you jest. The man has terrorized London with his bombs for years. Had you not been brought in by Mister Orr, it's impossible to say how much longer he might have continued."

"I'm not disputing the immorality of his actions, old friend. It's just that I have come to understand how badly his people have been treated. Thousands, perhaps hundreds of thousands of lives lost to starvation. In fact, there are some who believe as many as a million souls perished in the potato famine. Families were ripped apart. Men were transported to Australia for stealing food in order to feed their children.

"And at the same time, many of the English landlords demanded the rent be paid in full. I'm afraid the English, as a people, acted rather badly during that period."

"I agree with you. But that doesn't give Michael and his ilk the right to terrorize innocent citizens whose only fault is that they were born British."

"I quite agree, but when the government won't listen, what recourse is left?"

"I suppose we could debate this back and forth for days and never reach a conclusion, or even a compromise."

"You are right, old friend. But you know my methods – sometimes it helps to talk a problem through."

"I know you've done it with cases, and you've told me more than once that I make an excellent sounding board. However, in this instance, I can see no grey."

"Well, there is the fact that while his bombs injured a number of people – the only ones to have died were the bombers at the London Bridge."

"Don't forget the lad at Clerkenwell."

"I haven't forgot, but that was in 1867, so I'm not certain we can attribute that atrocity to Michael."

188

"I'll end my side of the debate with two more thoughts. First, you say no one perished but the bombers, and that is true. But I think we have to thank heaven that his explosives didn't do more damage or result in a serious loss of lives. You said there was an inexactness about the bombs. Whether one of his bombs detonated in an empty room or one filled with people does not appear to have concerned him. That no one was killed was more Divine Providence than grand design."

"And your second point?"

"At the Tower, just before Michael hurled the bomb at the ravens, I told him killing nuns and children wouldn't help his cause, and he looked at me and said, 'War demands sacrifices.' Those children weren't soldiers, and the only war Michael is fighting is the one in his mind."

With that, I lapsed into silence, and as I sat there ruminating, I hoped that I had given my friend something to consider. "Quandry, indeed!" I thought to myself.

After numerous stops and several naps, we finally arrived in Holyhead around nine o'clock. Holmes managed to find a cab and the driver took us to the docks. As we drove, he explained his plan to me. When he had finished, he said, "We will have only one shot at this, so we must hit the mark or our quarry will be gone forever."

"Which is the next mail packet leaving for Dublin?" Holmes inquired of a stevedore.

"That'd be the midnight ship – three piers down."

Although it was now May, we had not left the showers of April behind us. A fine mist was falling, and there seemed the imminent possibility of heavier rain in the hours ahead. We walked to the pier and I saw before me a ship straining at her ropes, seemingly eager to be off to her home country. The City of Dublin Steam Packet Company had won a contract to carry the mail from Wales to Dublin back in 1850. As a result, the company then had four steam packets built – the Connaught, the Ulster, the Munster and the Leinster, named for the provinces of Ireland. All of them bore the designation RMS or Royal Mail Ship. I looked to see which one we would be boarding and was surprised to see it was the Connaught. I wondered if that might be an omen of some sort.

When we reached the ship, Holmes purchased two tickets and said, "Let's board now. I want to have a few words with the captain."

The wind had started to pick up and I prepared myself for a rough crossing. We went below and found Captain Cornelius O'Sullivan discussing something with his first mate. Perhaps in his early fifties, the captain was a solid-looking man with a military bearing. Unfortunately, our interview got off to an inauspicious start when the first mate snapped, "You're not supposed to be here,"

"It's extenuating circumstances that bring me here." Holmes then introduced himself. I thought I detected a flicker of recognition in the captain's eyes, but I could see his name meant nothing to the mate.

Looking at the mate, Holmes said, "If you would excuse us, what I have to discuss with Captain O'Sullivan is a matter of some delicacy."

The mate looked angry and confused but the captain reassured him, "It's all right, Tommy."

After the mate departed, Holmes quickly outlined the events of the day, placing particular emphasis on the recent attempt the lives of on Prince Arthur and his wife. "The Duke of Connaught?" the captain exclaimed.

"Indeed," replied Holmes.

"How can you be certain they will be on this boat and not traveling from Liverpool?"

"Yours is the fastest ship between here and Ireland is it not?"

"Far and away, perhaps the only ship faster than mine is the Ireland. Still, under the right conditions, I'm certain we could give her a run for her money."

"And you can make the quickest crossing to Kingstown?"

"Aye."

"He will be on this boat. He is from Kingstown, and I am certain he's heading home to safety and those that will shelter him from the law."

Although it pained me to do so, I interrupted Holmes saying, "I think you are mistaken there, Holmes. I distinctly remember Michael telling us he was from Dunleavy."

Both Holmes and the captain smiled, "Watson, if anything, Michael said he was from Dunleary."

"Yes, that's it, Dunleary. Dunleary," I repeated, emphasizing the "r."

"You really must continue to brush up on your Irish history. The original name of Kingstown was Dunleary. It was changed in 1820 after a visit from King George IV. I am certain no self-respecting Irishman would refer to his birthplace by a name honoring an English monarch if there were another choice available."

Holmes then turned back to the captain, "If I may ask, how many passengers do you usually carry on your voyages to Kingstown?"

"It depends, sir. During the day in the summer, we can have as many as twenty or thirty. However, on these night runs in winter and spring, we may take as few as two or three – sometimes none."

"Has anyone boarded yet?" asked Holmes.

"Just you two," replied O'Sullivan.

Holmes looked at his watch. "It's now ten o'clock. What time do you plan to set sail?"

"We are scheduled to depart at midnight, but our departure time can vary slightly. We cannot sail until the mail train arrives, and the sacks have been placed on board. It's due in at midnight, and it doesn't take us long to get under way after that."

Holmes seemed satisfied with the answer. "Is there someplace where we can stay and observe who boards without being seen? If I am wrong, I have no desire to cross to Ireland tonight. In fact, my presence may be required elsewhere."

The captain installed us both in the onboard post office. "I don't think anyone will be mailing letters tonight, especially if the wind keeps picking up."

Settled in the small cabin, we had a clear view of the gangplank and if we remained in the shadows, we could not be seen by anyone coming aboard. The mist continued to fall, but it did not affect our visibility.

Time passed slowly and neither one of us wanted to take the chance of lighting a pipe or a cigarette. After about an hour, a man made his way aboard but he was far too short to be Michael. Fifteen minutes later, another man came on deck. Although, he was the right height and build, when he passed by the cabin, we were able to get a good look at his face, and it wasn't Michael.

At about five minutes before the hour, I heard a train whistle in the distance. "It would appear the mail train is right on time," said Holmes.

I wondered what Holmes would do if Michael failed to appear. Although I felt like asking, I decided to hold my tongue. A few minutes later, the mail train with smoke billowing from its stack huffed to a stop amid the shrieking of the brakes. I watched as a group of men began hauling bags from the train and entrusting them to sailors who began to bring them aboard.

After the last sack had been stowed below decks, I felt that unless we wanted to sail to Ireland, we should probably disembark. I was just about to speak when all of a sudden Holmes hissed, "There! Did you see him?"

As I peered into the darkness, I spied a figure darting from the shadows just as the crew members were about to cast off. Even through the glass, I could hear him pleading, "Wait! Wait!"

They placed the gangplank back on the deck, and a minute later Michael scampered up it, handed over his ticket and headed to the lounge below deck.

Before we got underway, the captain appeared at the door, and said, "So will you be sailing or disembarking?"

"I haven't been to Ireland in some time," replied Holmes. "How long does the voyage take?"

"Normally, we can make it in well under four hours, but tonight, with this weather, I'd be happy if we made it in four – let alone under."

"All we can hope is that it doesn't get too rough," I offered.

"Do you mind if we remain here for a while?" asked Holmes.

"Not at all. Is there anything else I can do?"

"If you could stop by when we are approximately halfway there, I might have one small request of you then."

"I certainly will, Mr. Holmes."

After the captain had left, Holmes turned to me and said in a tone that would brook no argument: "This will all be over soon."

Chapter 19

Some two hours later, the captain knocked on the window of the post office. Through the glass I could see him mouth the words "halfway home." After another minute or two, Holmes and I left the cabin and began walking along the deck. Out on the Irish Sea, the wind was howling and the rain was coming down in buckets. Under a bit of an overhang, we stood outside the porthole looking into the lounge. There were three men inside; two were sitting at one end, towards the front of the ship and Michael was sitting by himself at the opposite end of the room. He was slouched back and it appeared as though he might be trying to sleep.

It was a large room, perhaps forty feet long by twenty wide. There were two entrances so that one might enter or leave the room from either side of the ship. There were perhaps ten or twelve benches in the room, and they had been arranged so that except for the two end benches closest to the fore and aft walls, all the others faced each other in groups of two. This had been done so large groups could sit and face each other and carry on a conversation, were they so inclined.

Holmes then cupped his hands around my ear and said, "I'll go in first." He added, "Dressed as I am, I don't think Michael will recognise me straight off. You, however, are another case entirely." He then continued, telling me exactly what he wanted me to do. He concluded by saying, "Take no chances, old friend. This is a dangerous and desperate man we are confronting. When he realizes the game is up there is no telling what he may do."

I watched as Holmes entered the lounge and started towards the bench where Michael was sitting. When he was about ten feet away, I saw Michael's head turn as he cast a glance in that direction. I carefully made my way around the cabin and as quietly as possible entered the lounge through the other door with my collar up and my hat pulled low. I immediately turned away from Michael and I was pretty certain he hadn't seen me as his back was to me. In fact, I could swear he hadn't even turned his head in my direction.

I took a seat so that I was directly behind Michael, albeit in the middle of the room, with my back to him. The other two men were sitting in front of me and one had stretched out to sleep on the bench. The other was engrossed in his paper. I could see Holmes out of the corner of my eye. He sat on the same bench as Michael at the far end.

After a few minutes, I heard Holmes whisper in his Irish brogue, "Michael, are you awake?"

I heard Michael exclaim, "Fergus? Is that you? What are you doing here?" I cast a quick glance over my shoulder and saw Michael staring at Holmes. "Yer not Fergus!"

He then looked about the room and spotted me, "I see you brought your lapdog with you. Good evening, Hamish, or whatever your name might be."

Before I could reply, Holmes said, "My name is Sherlock Holmes."

"Holmes? I've heard of you," snarled Michael, "A Scotland Yard busybody, a snitch. Well, we're on the seas now, and you've got no jurisdiction over me here."

"You are quite correct," replied Holmes. "Still, I suspect you will wind up in an English prison eventually. You have committed any number of crimes, and you must answer for them."

"What about your part in the explosions? At Downing Street and Trevelyan's residence? You planted the bombs, boyo!"

"In both cases, those blasts were carefully staged. The only damage done was to a few of the front windows at 10 Downing and some stairs at Trevelyan's house."

"But the bombs you made? The lists you provided?"

"All part of a plan to bring you to heel and end your wretched campaign."

"End the campaign? End the campaign? Are ya daft? There were rough men before me who made and planted bombs and more of the same will come after me to continue the work. You'll not stop us because we'll not be stopped until Ireland is free."

"Michael, the police have already arrested most of your confederates."

"I notice you said most – not all?"

"We are looking for Daire, and we will find her."

"I think not, my friend. I was smart enough to let you think her a man, and I planned her escape far better than my own obviously. Tell the truth, you thought to catch us both together, didn't you?"

"I was rather hoping," admitted Holmes.

"Let me tell you something, Mr. Holmes. You may have captured me – although that remains to be seen – but Daire is free, and in her you have made a powerful enemy. When she finds out what role you have played in having my men arrested and learns you tried to arrest me as well, she will seek revenge. From now on, you had best be careful when opening your packages." He chuckled and then turning to me he added, "And you too."

"Perhaps if you were to provide her surname, the court might take your cooperation into consideration when you are sentenced," I said.

"As I sit here now, I swear you'll not be putting me in an English prison. Have you any idea what your English guards do to people such as me?"

When neither of us answered, he continued, "No? I thought not. They call the Irish prisoners they've captured so far the 'Special Men.' They are starved, beaten, humiliated, denied even the basic necessities, all in an attempt to break them. God willin', yer won't break me, but a man can take only so much, and I swear you'll not set yer boot on my neck."

"So you feel you've done nothing wrong?" asked Holmes.

"Do you feel the English have done anythin' wrong, Mr. Holmes? I'm a patriot. All I'm doing is paying you back in kind. If a few English people have been wounded, that doesn't even begin to equal the hundreds of thousands of Irish who starved to death because of you cruel bastards."

I am sure we could have debated this all night and probably longer. However, Michael suddenly repeated something he had said earlier, "You are not a police officer, are you Mr. Holmes? No, I thought not. So, you have no authority over me unless you are prepared to kidnap me and bind me in order to return me to England."

"You are right, Michael. I have no authority over you, but I think you will agree that the captain of this ship has jurisdiction over all of us while we are at sea. I've apprised him of your situation." Turning to me, Holmes said, "Watson. Would you be so kind as to see whether Captain O'Sullivan is free, and if he is, would you ask him to join us?"

I made my way to the bridge over the rain-slicked deck where I found the captain struggling with the wheel. After I had relayed Holmes' request, he turned over the wheel to his first mate. "I hope this won't take long," he said, "'Tis a rough night, indeed." He then accompanied me back to the salon.

When we entered, we stood next to Holmes, who said, "Thank you for joining us, Captain. This is the gentleman I discussed with you earlier. I would like you to detain him and then he, Watson and I will return to England with him by the first boat where I will turn him over to the proper authorities."

The captain looked at Michael and said, "Sir, under my authority as the captain of the RMS Connaught, I am taking you into custody to be returned to England on the next RMS boat."

"I must inform you, Captain, I do not recognize your authority. I should also caution you that any attempt to remove me from Ireland may well be met with resistance by my brothers-in-arms."

We had obviously reached an impasse, and I wondered if indeed Michael had wired ahead and asked for other revolutionaries to meet him at the pier.

There was a tense silence for a few minutes. Suddenly Michael spoke, "Since I may well be a condemned man, might I have a match and a cigarette from one of you?"

"Just a minute," I said, reaching into my pocket and stepping towards him with a box of vespers and my cigarettes.

"He doesn't smoke," yelled Holmes, who stopped me with his arm. "You wouldn't be carrying a stick of dynamite and hoping to light the fuse from your cigarette, would you, Michael?"

"Aren't you the sharp one?" Michael asked, pulling two sticks of dynamite from the inside of his coat. As he looked about a thought struck him? "Do you think you might be able to stop me from getting to the lantern and lighting the fuse? You wouldn't have much time if I succeeded, for it's a rather short fuse."

At that moment it struck me that Michael, while appearing calm and composed, was actually on the verge of hysteria. Knowing that, I realized there was no way of actually predicting what he might do next. I wondered how I might communicate my new-found knowledge to Holmes when he said, "Why don't we all just take a seat and see if we can't come to some sort of reasonable compromise?"

He then took off his coat and proceeded to turn to Captain O'Sullivan. Indicating the two men at the front of the cabin who were now facing us and watching everything intently – apparently, our words had awakened the sleeping one at some point – Holmes said to O'Sullivan, "Might I suggest you escort those gentlemen either to the post office or the wheelhouse, whichever you feel is safer."

"Gentlemen, if you would accompany me, I think we might be able to find something to warm your innards on a night like this." The three of them then left the lounge, and then it was just Michael, Holmes and me. For a moment I thought of all the nights we had conversed in the Ten Bells, but this was nothing like that.

"So what do you propose, Mr. Holmes?"

"First, you might consider returning the dynamite to your coat pocket."

"I think not. For even I can see that Hamish is armed. Perhaps if he places his pistol on the bench at the far end of the room, I'll be more inclined to talk."

Holmes nodded at me, and I did as Michael had requested.

"Leave yer coat there as well. After all, while the gun in the right pocket gives it away, I've no idea what might be in yer left – now, do I?"

After that I sat between Holmes and Michael, and for thirty minutes or so, they debated the thorny problem that was freedom for Ireland. Listening to Michael, I began to understand fully how his people had suffered and the resentment they felt towards anything or anyone English.

It was a give-and-take and I wondered if Holmes were making any progress in persuading Michael to surrender peacefully. During a lull in the conversation, Michael asked, "Do you know what time it is?"

I looked at my watch and told him it was not quite half two. He smiled enigmatically and then said, "I have but one regret about this whole affair."

Since Holmes was busy tamping his pipe, I simply said, "Oh? What might that be?"

"That I will not join my parents in Glasnevine."

I was about to ask, "Where is that?" when Holmes bellowed, "Grab him, Watson, Don't let him get away."

Michael had risen and turned to run up the side aisle to the closest door. The best I could do was grab the arm of his coat but he slipped out of it and I was left holding an empty garment. Although Holmes was now running towards the door, Michael was out it before my friend could reach him. Following hard behind, I thought I heard a splash and then Holmes began to yell, "Man overboard! Man overboard!"

A few minutes later, the ship came to a stop, and Captain O'Sullivan appeared beside us on the deck. "What happened?"

"He jumped in," replied Holmes.

The captain and the mates "halloed" and held out lanterns attached to long poles. However, they searched in vain, for there was no sign of Michael.

After about ten minutes, the captain said, "In this water, he wouldn't last more than five or ten minutes. I'm afraid we've lost him, Mr. Holmes."

"I understand, Captain."

He then left us and a few minutes later we were under speed again.

"Did you know he was going to commit suicide?" I asked.

"No, old friend. I actually thought we were making progress."

"What gave him away?"

"When he said he wanted to join his parents in Glasnevin."

"I still don't understand."

"Glasnevin is the first and largest Catholic cemetery in Ireland."

It was a sobering thought, and to some small degree I blamed myself for Michael's death. Had I been more thorough in studying the history of Ireland, I might have picked up on it, reacted sooner and saved his life.

As if reading my mind. Holmes attempted to console me saying, "You can't blame yourself, Watson. Michael made a choice. Now, let us see what steps we can take to make certain his death was not in vain."

Chapter 20

It was three days later, and Holmes and I were sitting in our rooms at Baker Street. My beard was gone, and I was freshly scrubbed. In short, I felt like a new man, having resumed my old life.

The afternoon was slowly giving way to evening, and I was preparing to assemble my notes on this case.

As I sat at my desk, staring at a blank sheet of foolscap, Holmes suddenly interrupted my thoughts. "I have a suggestion for you, and a request."

"Oh?"

"If you are planning to write up our most recent case, you might want to put off beginning until tomorrow, or at least until later this evening."

"Why is that?"

"Lestrade is going to stop by after dinner, and Mr. Orr has promised to visit us at eight. They may be able to provide something of a denouement for this tragic tale."

"That's certainly true," I said. "And the request?"

"Assuming no one else has any objections, I would ask you not to publish the account of the Irish bombers until I too have shuffled off this mortal coil."

"Why would you ask such a thing?"

"As I said this is a tragic case. There is injustice on both sides; all we have done is put a halt to one side's inequity – and probably only a temporary halt at that. Plus, as I told you, I have been criminally slow in arriving at certain conclusions. No, old friend, there will be no accolades for anyone involved in this case." After a pause, he added, "Except perhaps, of course, for Scotland Yard."

I could do little but smile.

After a meal that was spent in a desultory silence, Holmes and I had taken our seats by the fire and were enjoying cigars and brandy in an amiable silence when I heard the front doorbell ring.

"That must be Lestrade, punctual as ever," remarked Holmes.

A few seconds later, I heard the inspector's distinctive footfalls on the stairs and then a rather loud knocking on the door.

"Come in, Lestrade," yelled Holmes.

The inspector entered our rooms, wearing a large smile. "Good evening, Mr. Holmes, Dr. Watson. I have a great deal to thank you for," he said."

"Oh?" asked Holmes innocently.

"Based on information supplied in large part by you, we rounded up most of the Fenian bombers,"

"Most?" I inquired.

"Their leader, a fellow named Michael, managed to escape as did one or two low-level soldiers, I guess you'd call them. We did nab Michael's right-hand man, a chap named Jimmy, and several other conspirators. Also, when we searched a house on Turner Street, we discovered a number of bombs in a trunk.

"But even more surprising was the fact that we recovered a number of items that had been stolen from the various shops I approached you about some while back.

"I'm guessing that is why you wouldn't help me at the time. Am I right?"

Holmes ignored his question and said, "Would you care for a brandy, Inspector?"

Of course Lestrade accepted and for the next forty minutes, Holmes gave him a brief synopsis of our actions over the past few months. As you might expect, a great many details were omitted – for any number of reasons – but when he had finished, Lestrade seemed satisfied.

"Oh, there is one more thing, Lestrade. You need not concern yourself with Michael any longer."

"Do you know where he is?"

"Not exactly," replied Holmes, "but I can assure you that he will pose no further threat to the people of London."

"Well, that's good news, if I say so myself." He then gave Holmes a knowing look.

We chatted for a few more minutes and then Lestrade said he had to be going. After the inspector had departed, I looked at Holmes and said, "That was a rather imprecise recitation of our recent adventures you shared with the good inspector."

"I told him everything he needed to know to complete his investigation. I think even you would have to agree that some things are best left unsaid."

Perhaps fifteen minutes later just as the clock was striking eight, I heard the front doorbell. Mrs. Hudson soon knocked on our door, "Please Mrs. Hudson, show Mr. Orr in."

She opened the door and once again Robert Orr, first deputy to Assistant Commissioner James Monro, stepped into our rooms.

206

"Mr. Holmes, Dr. Watson, let me begin by thanking you both. From the reports I have received, the bombing ring has been dealt with and many of its members arrested."

"*This* bombing ring," said Holmes by way of clarifying the statement. "Another may yet rise to take its place."

"Let us hope we have arrived at some sort of reconciliation before that comes to pass," said Orr.

"I would hope the body politic can see its way clear to either giving the Irish home rule or granting them their independence. The system we currently have is both untenable and inequitable, and those wrongs must be redressed."

I think Orr was stunned by my friend's directness and he mumbled something to the effect of, "I'm sure you are correct."

There followed an uncomfortable silence which was finally broken when Orr said, "Oh, by the way, Mr. Holmes, the Prime Minister has been apprised of your labours, and he asked me to give you this as a small token of his appreciation." With that he reached into his pocket and withdrew an envelope which he handed to Holmes. Holmes thanked him and then without opening it, he folded the envelope and thrust it deep into the pocket of his jacket, which had replaced his dressing gown just prior to the arrival of Mr. Orr.

"Please extend my thanks to the Prime Minister, and tell him such a gesture is appreciated although it is totally unnecessary."

"Well, I must be going," said Orr, "I have a meeting at seven in the morning."

I walked him to the door and when I returned Holmes was standing at the window. He turned and thrust the envelope in my direction. "Take this and see if you can find a reputable Irish charity seeking donations."

"I'm certain there are dozens of them," I replied.

"Choose any one you like; just see that the money is spent to help those people who have suffered at the hands of our people."

As you might expect the check was considerable, and I ended up giving equal shares to three different organizations.

Holmes spoke of this particular case on only one other occasion. A few months later an article appeared in *The Times* remarking on the seeming end of the Fenian bombing campaign, and the fact that the people of London no longer had to live in fear.

At the risk of stirring up unpleasant memories, I remarked on it at lunch that day.

Holmes smiled at me and said, "I have often thought of that case and in particular the long discussion we had with Michael on the boat. He said one thing that has stuck with me, and the more I reflect upon it, the more I realize how true it is.

"What remark was that, Holmes?"

"During our discussion on the boat, he quoted Giordano Bruno, the Italian astronomer, philosopher and mathematician who was burned at the stake in Rome in 1600 on charges of heresy. Immediately after he had been convicted and sentenced to death, Bruno told his accusers, 'Perchance you who pronounce my sentence are in greater fear than I who receive it.'"

"Surely you are not equating a mad bomber with a Renaissance scientist."

"They share a great many similarities. Think about it some time, and if you should ever decide to chronicle this adventure, I pray you to include that quote. I think your readers may find it most enlightening."

Epilogue

5 June, 1916

As I sit here reading of the outcome of the Easter Rising in Ireland, I am reminded of an observation once made by my dear friend, Sherlock Holmes, many years ago. As we were investigating that case I titled *The Valley of Fear,* Holmes said to me, "Everything comes in circles. ... The old wheel turns, and the same spoke comes up. It's all been done before and will be again."

As you have just learned, Holmes and I were instrumental in foiling a Fenian bombing plot in the mid-1880s. At the time, I remember Holmes fearing that another bomber would simply replace the one who had been lost. Such was not the case, and for many years London lived free of the spectre of the sudden explosion.

However, as I read of the rebellion in Ireland, I am saddened to think that so little has been learned from the past. Yes, there were attempts made in both 1886 and 1893 to secure more rights for Ireland. Sadly, the First Home Rule Bill, introduced to Parliament by Charles Stewart Parnell, was soundly defeated. Seven years later, the Second Home Rule Bill was introduced and passed by the House of Commons. Unfortunately, it was rejected by the House of Lords.

Even the influence of Prime Minister H.H. Asquith, who introduced a Third Home Rule Bill in 1912, was not sufficient to bring peace to that troubled land. Asquith's bill was vehemently opposed by Irish Unionists, who were overwhelmingly Protestant, and feared living under a Catholic-dominated Irish government.

The missteps and duplicity that led to the Easter Rising could fill a book and possibly several, so I will not detail them any further here. What I will say is that meeting farmers and shopkeepers with a trained army, supported by gun boats and nearly unlimited resources has never been anyone's idea of fair play.

While executing the leaders may serve to dissuade others for the moment, those people have also been transformed into martyrs. I can look down the road and see the same wheel spinning over and over again, until the question of Irish freedom is resolved.

I believe there is a spark within man that understands certain things are inviolate – and personal freedom is certainly at the top of that list. When one's liberty is restricted or ignored and his rights trampled on, what choice does he have but to strike back?

Again, I have not and do not condone the bombings, but I have come to a greater understanding of the lengths to which men will go when they are pushed beyond their limits.

Perhaps what makes the English-Irish situation even worse is the fact that the source of much of this trouble is a difference in religion. The party in power sees nothing wrong with subjugating others, but if there is a chance that the roles will be reversed … well we end up back where we have been. The wheel has turned.

I do not know how the Easter Rising will finally resolve itself and what shape the next generation of Irish rebels will take, but I can say with some degree of certainty that unless the differences which separate us are resolved, we can expect more of the same in the future.

Given the enormous progress of the past few decades – flying machines, automobiles and wireless communication, to name just a few – arriving at a means of reconciliation ought to be child's play.

I say it ought to be child's play and while I hope that I am correct, deep in my soul, I fear that I am wrong.

– John H. Watson, M.D.

Author's Notes

The relationship between England and Ireland is a long and tumultuous affair. This book does not attempt to explain nor explore that contentious history. Rather I have focused on a series of events in the 1880s which have become known as the "Fenian Dynamite Campaign."

The bombings started long before 1884, when this book opens, but for any number of reasons they ceased for many years after 1885.

The incidents outlined in the opening chapters – the attempted bombing of the London Bridge, the explosive devices which were detonated at the House of Commons, Tower of London, and Westminster Hall – all took place as did all the other earlier explosions.

For the full story of the campaign, I'd suggest reading Joseph McKenna's *The Irish-American Dynamite Campaign: A History 1881-1896.* It is a fascinating look at that tumultuous time.

The doss houses of Whitechapel were an abomination. Hundreds of people sleeping in a room with inadequate facilities. The history of those places makes for compelling, if somewhat disturbing, reading and the fee for a bed for a night – four pence – was what many of the prostitutes in Whitechapel charged. That way they knew at least they'd have a roof over their heads for the evening.

The Ten Bells is one of London's oldest pubs. The name of the pub has changed over time, but those names have generally been derived from the number of bells in the "peal" housed in nearby Christ Church. Most people associate the pub and Whitechapel with Jack the Ripper and according to legend, at least two of the Ripper's victims had their last drink there. In fact between 1976 and 1988, the pub was called "The Jack the Ripper."

Just about all of the other pubs mentioned in the book existed in 1885, and a number of them are still in business today. The Brown Bear can trace its history to the beginning of the 18th century while The White Hart was founded in 1721.

When Lestrade visits Holmes about the spate of robberies, the inspector mentions the Forty Elephants. They were an all-female gang that engaged in robbery, shoplifting and ransacking the homes in which they had taken positions in service. The gang continued up until the 1950s.

Sir Charles Edward Trevelyan was a career politician. He was reviled among the Irish for his actions, or lack thereof, during the height of the famine. He was slow to disburse direct government food and monetary aid to the Irish due to his strong belief in *laissez-faire* economics and the free hand of the market. He also wrote highly disparaging remarks about the Irish in a letter to an Irish peer, stating that "the judgement [sic} of God sent the calamity to teach the Irish a lesson."

The legend of the ravens at the Tower of London has many sources and just as many variations. For this work, I accepted a rather straightforward version and ignored the numerous embellishments.

Finally, the RMS Connaught was a real ship ferrying mail from Holyhead to Dublin. It could make the crossing in well under four hours. As I mentioned in the book, it and its three sister ships were known as "The Provinces."

214

Acknowledgments

I still maintain that writing, at least as I practice it, is a lonely task. Over the years, I've gotten into the habit of writing late at night when everyone is in bed and the house is still. However, it has been made somewhat less onerous by the encouragement and patience of friends and family, especially my wife, who have supported and cheered me on in my endeavors.

I should be terribly remiss if I failed to thank my publisher, Steve Emecz, who makes the process painless, and the enormously talented Brian Belanger, whose skill as a cover designer is unmatched.

No book is complete without a solid line edit, and Deborah Annakin Peters continues to provide that as well as a number of invaluable suggestions all of which improve my books immeasurably. She also makes certain that my Britishisms are correct and that no Americanisms creep in. My works are so much better because of her diligence and care.

I also owe a considerable debt to Dr. Robert Katz, a good friend, who remains the finest Sherlockian I know. He has continued to encourage me and is kind enough to read my efforts with an eye toward accuracy – both with regard to the Canon, and perhaps more importantly, to common sense.

To Francine and Richard Kitts, two outstanding Sherlockians, for their unflagging support and encouragement. Both of whom were kind enough to read the manuscript in its raw form and suggest improvements.

To my brother, Edward; and my sister, Arlene; who continue to believe in me even when I am constantly doubting myself.

I owe a special debt to many of my former students both at Moore Catholic and St. Peter's Boys who have read and enjoyed my books and offered kind words of encouragement. You know who you are, and I can't thank you enough.

Finally, to all those, and there are far too many to name, whose support for my earlier efforts have made me see just what a wonderful life I have and what great people I am surrounded by. So to all those who have read my earlier works, a sincere thank you.

To say that I am in the debt of all those mentioned here doesn't even begin to scratch the surface of my gratitude.

Finally, if there are errors in this book – and I'm pretty sure there are – the only person responsible for them is me.

About the author

Richard T. Ryan is a native New Yorker, having been born and raised on Staten Island. He majored in English at St. Peter's College (now St. Peter's University) in Jersey City and pursued his graduate studies, concentrating on medieval literature, at the University of Notre Dame in Indiana.

After teaching high school and college for more than a decade, he joined the staff of the Staten Island Advance newspaper. He worked there for nearly 30 years, rising through the ranks to become news editor. When he retired in 2016, he held the position of publications manager for that paper although he still prefers the title, news editor.

In addition to his first novel, "The Vatican Cameos: A Sherlock Holmes Adventure," he has written "The Stone of Destiny: A Sherlock Holmes Adventure," "The Druid of Death," "The Merchant of Menace," "Through a Glass Starkly," "Three May Keep a Secret" and "The Poisoned Pawn." Five of his novels have been published in Italian by Mondadori.

Other published works include "B Is for Baker Street: My First Sherlock Holmes Book," which he wrote for his grandchildren, Riley Grace and Henry Robert. He has also penned three trivia books, including "The Official Sherlock Holmes Trivia Book."

Wearing a different hat, he serves as the editor for the *Year in Mystery* series for Belanger Books, which attempts to fill in the voids in the Sherlockian Canon. The first four books, 1881 through 1884, are available and the fifth and sixth volumes are due out later this year. Also for Belanger Books, he has co-edited *Writing Holmes,* a collection of essay on why and how people write about the world's Greatest Detective. He is also co-editing *Reading Holmes* as well as editing *No Holidays for Holmes*, a collection of short stories.

In a slightly different medium, he can also boast at having *Deadly Relations*, a mystery-thriller produced off-Broadway on two separate occasions at the Playwrights Horizons Theatre.

And if that weren't enough, he is the very proud father of two children, Dr. Kaitlin Ryan-Smith and Michael Ryan, and the incredibly proud grandfather of the aforementioned Riley Grace and Henry Robert.

He has been married for 45 years to his wife, Grace, and continues to marvel at her incredible patience in putting up with him and his computer illiteracy.

He is currently at work on his ninth novel, a period piece set in the Middle Ages, which just keeps getting put off by Holmes stories. After finishing that, if he ever does, he plans to take another look into the box he purchased at auction and see what tales remain.

Keep reading for an excerpt from Richard T. Ryan's next book:

The Tortured Templar:
A Sherlock Holmes Adventure

By Richard Ryan

Chapter 1

It was a fine spring morning, and Sherlock Holmes was indulging in one of his favorite pastimes. Standing at the window overlooking Baker Street, he would watch the comings and goings of the throngs traversing the thoroughfare below. He would then select some passerby who had caught his attention, and begin to analyse that man or woman's dress, gait, complexion and other pertinent facts in an effort to ascertain the individual's occupation and the business that had brought him or her hither. As you might expect, he was seldom wrong regarding these types of deductions.

I was reading the paper when my thoughts were suddenly interrupted as Holmes exclaimed, "Hallo! What have we here? A fine Clarence with matching stallions. The driver is obviously looking for a house number – and he appears to have found it." After a few seconds he turned to me and said, "Unless I am very much mistaken, a new client has come to seek our assistance – one with whom I have some slight acquaintance."

Doffing his dressing gown and donning his frock coat, Holmes then proceeded to collect several piles of papers that had been strewn about the floor, concealing them behind the settee. Knowing how totally unconcerned with appearances Holmes was as a rule, I thought, "This must be some dignitary or potentate. After all, Sherlock Holmes doesn't tidy up the flat for just anybody."

A minute or two later, I heard the doorbell ring and shortly after that, Mrs. Hudson knocked on the door. "Come in, Mrs. Hudson," said Holmes.

Our landlady entered and said, "A gentleman to see you, sir." After handing Holmes, the man's card, she offered, "He says it is a matter of some urgency, sir."

"Show him up, dear lady. And if you would be so kind, perhaps you might bring up a pot of tea and perhaps a few biscuits if any are available."

I was rather taken aback at Holmes' courtliness, and I began to wonder who this visitor might be. I hadn't long to wait as just a moment later, a nervous-looking man in his mid-thirties tentatively knocked on the open door. He was of medium height and medium build with fair hair and slight moustache. He seemed altogether an unprepossessing individual which made Holmes' actions seem that much stranger.

"Come in," said Holmes. "Please take a seat," he said indicating one of the wing chairs by the hearth.

"I do hope I haven't come at an inopportune time, Mr. Holmes," he explained, but the matter is most pressing – at least to me it is." Having made this pronouncement, he sat and fidgeted as he waited for Holmes to speak.

After a few seconds when Holmes remained silent, he began, "My name is Ronald Holborn, and I serve as the –."

Holmes cut him off, "I am well aware of who you are, sir, and of your position as head curator with the Wallace Collection.

I also know that you keep a small brindle terrier, prefer marmalade jam and enjoy painting landscapes as a hobby."

Holborn looked astounded at Holmes' pronouncements, but I had seen those tricks before. Looking closer, I could discern a slight smudge of jam on the outside of his left cuff and the dog hair stood out against the cuffs of his light grey trousers, but how Holmes had arrived at the painting escaped me. Looking up, I saw that Holmes was watching me and he smiled ever so slightly.

"Still, you didn't come here to discuss your personal life, so what has upset you to the point that you feel as though you need my assistance?"

"I can only assume that you have visited the collection since it so close by."

"Indeed, I have been there on any number of occasions – usually for research but now and then for pleasure. I am quite fond of Franz Hals' *The Laughing Cavalier,* but again, you aren't here to discuss my fondness for the Dutch masters. So how may I help you?"

"As you know, the Wallace Collection has a rather extensive array of arms and armor, dating from the medieval period up to and including the present day."

"Indeed, I once had occasion to borrow a broadsword from the Collection, but that was some time ago before it was bequeathed to the nation and subsequently opened as a museum."

"And that's the strangest part of it, Mr. Holmes."

"Of what, exactly?" asked Holmes.

"The break-ins. As you observed, the museum is open to the public, yet I am quite certain that we are being frequented by a nocturnal visitor who surreptitiously visits the Collection late at night."

"As far as you know, has anything been taken?"

"Nothing. For the most part everything is exactly as it was when we closed the previous evening."

"Let us start at the beginning. When did you first decide the Collection was entertaining an untimely guest?"

"Suspicions were first raised perhaps a month ago. One of the docents discovered tallow drippings in front of a display of swords and shields in the first of the European Armory rooms."

"If memory serves there are three rooms in which European weapons and armor are displayed and a fourth in which Oriental arms are emphasized."

"Quite right, Mr. Holmes, The first time anyone noticed the drippings was in that first armory room which is located near the rear of Hertford House. As I am certain you will recall the room is dedicated to Medieval and Renaissance Arms and Armour, dating from the 10th to the 16th centuries. Several days later, we discovered similar drippings in the second European room, but both the third European room and the Oriental Armory appear to have been spared."

"When did all this begin?" I asked.

"It was perhaps the second week in April," Holborn replied.

"And how many times can you say for certain this visitor has sneaked into the Collection?" asked Holmes, anticipating my next question.

"At least four times – three times we have found drippings from either a candle or a dark lantern, and on the fourth occasion, the intruder appears to have dropped a small coin."

"The tallow droppings, where was the third?" Holmes asked.

"That was also found near the medieval armour," replied Holborn.

"And the coin? Where was it and what can you tell me about it?"

"The coin was discovered early this morning, which is why I am here. A member of the maintenance crew who was dusting the exhibits prior to opening came across it on a shelf in one of the display cases in the medieval armour room."

"Is it possible the coin was dropped on one of the earlier visits and simply not discovered until this morning?"

"It is certainly possible but unlikely I think as the items are dusted regularly, and the coin is shiny enough that I am certain it would have been spotted."

"So on three out of four occasions, the intruder appears to have spent time in the first European Armour room.

Obviously, there is something there that appears to have captured his attention."

"Did you bring the coin with you?"

"No, I had the worker replace it in the exact spot where he discovered it."

"Bravo!" exclaimed Holmes. "I should like very much to examine that room although I am not optimistic," said Holmes.

"Because of the visitors?" I inquired.

"Exactly," replied my friend.

"Well, you needn't worry about that, Mr. Holmes. I closed the room to the public before the museum opened. You see, I am somewhat familiar with your preferences and methods." With that, he gave me a knowing look.

"Excellent!" exclaimed Holmes, smiling at the man. I very much fear you may have missed your vocation, Mr. Holborn. Would that Scotland Yard took as much care to preserve a crime scene as you appear to have done."

"Are you certain there has been a crime?" I asked.

"At the very least, we have four occasions of breaking and entering. What other charges may be added to those remains to be seen. Now, Watson, if you have nothing else to occupy your day, let us make haste to get to the Wallace Collection."

"My carriage is waiting downstairs, gentlemen," said Holborn. And so it was that a few minutes later the three of us were headed toward Manchester Square. After the short ride, we entered through the rear, and Holborn explained that the European Armour was housed in what had once been the stables.

The doors to the room had been locked and a small velvet rope stood before them with a sign proclaiming, "Closed for Renovations."

Holborn took out a key and opened the doors. As soon as we entered, I was struck by the sheer number of weapons and suits of armour on display. In the middle of the room were several large cases filled with helms, gauntlets, swords, shields and dirks. Each case had been divided in half from side to side so that visitors could view different items depending upon which side they stood to look at the case.

The walls on both sides of the room contained even more display cases. The smaller ones housed entire suits of armour with various accoutrements while the larger ones focused on specific weapons and pieces of armour. One contained an astonishing array of broadswords and gauntlets while another boasted a selection of breastplates, helms, knives and other paraphernalia.

Holmes and I followed Holborn to one of the cabinets in the middle displaying swords and shields. After selecting a key from his ring, Holborn was about to open the cabinet when Holmes stopped him. "The coin was found inside the cabinet, you said," he stated.

"Indeed, that's what makes it so strange. Had it been found on the floor, it might not have been given a second thought but when the worker moved the shield to dust it, he discovered it laying behind it on the shelf."

"And you're certain that it wasn't there before?"

"Indeed, Mr. Holmes. I had but a moment to examine it, but it appears to be quite old." He then turned to open the cabinet, but Holmes asked him to wait a moment. He then knelt on the floor in front of the lock and pulling his lens from his pocket began to examine it in some detail. "There appear to be fresh scratches," he said almost to himself.

After a few moments, he stood and turning to Holborn, said, "Now, if you would, please open the cabinet."

Holborn did as he was bade and pulled open a wide glass door.

"Which shield was it found behind?" asked Holmes.

Holborn pointed to a partially hidden badge shield that was mostly obscured by a larger round shield. Holborn removed the larger shield and we could see that the small badge shield had been divided into quarters. The upper left and lower right featured a red cross against a white background. (I later learned that in heraldry red is referred to as "gules.") The other two quarters featured a gold band running diagonally, from the upper left to the lower right, against a background of blue or azure.

"Are you aware of the provenance of this shield?" asked Holmes.

"I believe it was acquired by Sir Richard Wallace in 1871, when he bought the collections of the Comte Alfred Emilien de

Nieuwekerke, Minister of Fine Arts to Napoleon III and director of the Louvre, as well as the finest parts of the collection of Sir Samuel Rush Meyrick, a pioneering collector and scholar of arms and armour."

"Yes, yes, I'm sure that's all very interesting to scholars and academics. The only part that interests me is that it appears the shield quite possibly came from France."

"Is that important, Holmes?" I asked.

"Perhaps. Beyond its acquisition, can you provide any further information about the shield?"

"I'm afraid not, Mr. Holmes. My area of expertise is late 17th and early 18th century French furniture with a particular emphasis upon the work of André -Charles Boulle."

Turning to me, Holmes rolled his eyes and while he found the answer annoying, he remained cordial when he said to Holborn, "So beyond what you have told us, you know nothing else about the shield?"

"I'm afraid not, Mr. Holmes," he answered.

"Holmes, it is quite obvious something about this shield has struck a note with you. Would you care to enlighten the rest of us?"

Holmes smiled and said, "Unless, I am very much mistaken, we are looking at a shield that may have once belonged to Jacques de Molay."

Although the name sounded vaguely familiar, I couldn't pin it down.

Fortunately, neither could Holborn who admitted, "I'm afraid I don't know that name."

"Jacques de Molay was a French Crusader who was burned at the stake in 1314 after being tortured and confessing to what many believe were trumped up charges that included blasphemy and heresy. However, more important than that is the fact that de Molay was the last Grand Master of the Knights Templar."

Milton Keynes UK
Ingram Content Group UK Ltd.
UKHW020933181023
430840UK00013B/446